D1593611

NAPOLEON
How to Make War

This edition is based on texts assembled by
Yann Cloarec for Éditions Champ Libre, published
in Paris in 1973 under the title *Comment faire la guerre*.
Used by permission of the publisher.

Translation and original essay "Postcards
from the Berezina" by Keith Sanborn

Contents of entire volume:
© Ediciones La Calavera 1998
ISBN: 0-9642284-2-4

Ediciones La Calavera
P.O. Box 1106
Peter Stuyvesant Station
New York, NY 10009

Editorial Board: Peggy Ahwesh,
Jayne Austen, Keith Sanborn

NAPOLEON
How to Make War

Texts assembled by Yann Cloarec

Translated by Keith Sanborn

EDICIONES LA CALAVERA

This translation is dedicated
to the life and work of Matthew Ward

*To the impudence there would be in prefacing
Napoleon, we prefer the humility of a statement. Let it be
said once again that as exporter of the capitalist mode of
production (and of the set of political relations which is
attached to it, the nation), Napoleon—without waiting for
Marx, but in pursuit of Destutt de Tracy, who forged
towards 1796 the concept of ideology—created, in order to
mock it, the noun ideologue: to reread Scott and Scheler
in this connection would not be without its uses. Let it next
be recalled that the reign of Napoleon coincides with the
disjoining of the pair ideology/strategy which, from 1803,
takes on the sense that currently occupies those women
and men whose ambition it is to accomplish revolution: to
import in dialectical fashion the principles of a war among
States is their task. Let it finally be repeated that history
does nothing: it is the real living man who does.*

—Y.C.

I remark with discomfort that there is, in your letter, a certain amount of infatuation and infatuation is very dangerous.

General rule: never a social revolution without terror. Every revolution of this nature is and can only be, in principle, a revolt; time and favorable results alone supervene to ennoble it, to render it legitimate; but once again, one could arrive at this only by means of terror. How can one say to all those who fill up all the administrative organs, hold all the posts, enjoy all the riches: Get out! It is clear that they would defend themselves; it is thus necessary to strike them with terror, to put them into flight, and it is this which lamppost justice and popular executions have accomplished.

In any case, a revolution is one of the greatest ills with which heaven can afflict the earth. It is the scourge of the generation that carries it out, all the advantages that it procures can hardly be worth the trouble with which it fills the lives of its authors.

What good is a maxim that can never be put into practice and that, once put into practice, should often be the cause of the ruin of the army.

I. General Principles

The affections change reason,
and the rules of a true politics
are the only things that never change.

1

The theory is not the practice of war.[1]

2

The art of war is a simple art and all in the execution; there is nothing vague in it, everything in it is common sense, nothing in it is ideology.

3

Words are everything.

4

War is a matter of opinion.

5

Everything is opinion in war, opinion about the enemy, opinion about one's own soldiers. After a lost battle, the difference between the vanquished and the victor is very little.

6

There is no need to say what one has the intention of doing at the same moment that one does it.

7

The art of war has unchanging principles which have
as their principal objective, the guaranteeing of armies
against the error of their leaders concerning the strength of
the enemy; an error which, more or less, always takes
place.

8

Every operation should be carried out according to
a system, because nothing succeeds by means of chance.
In war, nothing is obtained except by calculation; anything
which is not deeply thought through in the details never
produces any result. In war, simple and precise ideas
are needed.

9

Having a political system does not mean allowing
oneself to be dragged along by every event.

10

It is not for an event to govern politics, but for politics
to govern events.

11

When one begins to acquire the habit of action, one holds in contempt all theories and one makes use of them as do geometers, not in order to march in a straight line, but in order to continue in the same direction.

12

Everything that is only fantasy and that is not founded on true interest will not resist a reversal.[2]

13

In war, one must never do by one's own free will something worse than what could happen by itself

14

Nothing can be absolute in war.

15

Generals-in-chief are guided by their own experience or by their genius. Tactics, maneuvers, the science of the engineer and of the artillerist can be learned from treatises more or less like geometry; but knowledge of the higher aspects of war can be acquired only through experience, through the study of the history of wars and of the battles of

the great captains. Does one learn by studying grammar
how to compose a book of *The Iliad*, a tragedy of Corneille?

16

In war, the first principle of the general-in-chief is to
hide what he does, to see whether he has the means to
surmount the obstacles, and to do everything possible to
surmount them when he has so resolved.

17

It is always a troublesome thing to allow the public
to become aware of discussions among the highest echelons
of the authorities. One should always obey the higher
authority, except in order to bring about the presentation to
the government of the objections that one would judge it
appropriate to make.

18

Success in war depends on the prudence, the proper
conduct and the experience of the general.

19

An army is nothing, except through its head.

20

In war, the commander alone understands the importance of certain things, and can alone, by his will and by his higher lights, conquer and surmount all difficulties.

21

A collective government has less simple ideas and is longer to make decisions.

22

Never hold a council of war, but take the advice of each in private.

23

A man of war must have as much character as intelligence; men who have a great deal of intelligence and little character are the least well suited; it is like a ship with masts too far out of proportion with its ballast; it is better to have a great deal of character and little intelligence. Men, who are of but mediocre intelligence and a proportionate character, often succeed in this profession; what is needed is as much base as height. A general who has a great deal of intelligence and character in the same degree—this is Caesar, Hannibal, Prince Eugène, and Frederick.

24

In the profession of war as in letters, each has his genre.

25

The least one may require of administrative services is that soldiers fight with equal arms; that is the first duty of a minister and nothing justifies his not fulfilling it; do we not have enough disadvantages without that of armament? "If's" and "but's" justify nothing. An administrator is not responsible for events. A minister may not be justified for anything, he must succeed; there is for him no other rule.

26

One must be slow in deliberations and quick in execution.

27

Make few proclamations and avoid having put in the newspapers those acts of yours which are purely administrative. This great publicity, of which the newspapers of Europe seize hold, has more inconveniences than advantages.

28

The art of war consists of gaining time when one has inferior forces.

29

Courage is required to fight against strength, even more is sometimes required to admit one's weakness.

30

Besides, a wise and prudent man never increases the number of his enemies.

31

The art of war consists, with an inferior army, of always having more forces than one's enemy at the point where one attacks or at the point which is attacked; but this art is learned neither from books, nor through habit, it is a sense of conduct that properly constitutes genius in war.

32

The art of war is to dispose one's troops in such a way that they are everywhere at once. The art of the placement of troops is the great art of war. Always place your troops in such a manner that, whatever the enemy may do, you may always within a few days find yourself assembled.

33

The strength of an army, like the quantity of momentum in mechanics, is evaluated as the mass multiplied by the velocity.

34

The greatest means, when scattered about, produce no results, in artillery as in cavalry, in infantry, in fortifications, and in the entire military system.

35

In order not to be surprised by obtaining victories, one has only to think about defeats.

36

Do not make a frontal attack on positions you can obtain by turning.

37

Do not do what the enemy wants, for the sole reason that he desires it; avoid the battlefield that he has reconnoitered, studied, and with even more care the one that he has fortified and where he has entrenched himself.

38

War being a profession of execution, all complicated combinations should be put aside. Simplicity is the first condition of all good maneuvers.

39

I shall be accused of temerity, not of slowness, still one must have in one's favor the odds given by calculation.

40

Your letter, besides, contains too much intelligence. It is not necessary in war; what is necessary is exactitude, character, and simplicity.

41

Everything in life is a problem, it is only by means of the known that one can arrive at the unknown.

42

What more constitutes a people than an army? The general who does not know how to move it emotionally would be deprived of the most important of necessary qualities.

43

Men are what one wants them to be.

44

We want to believe that no officer would be so vile as
to abuse the ignorance of the soldier. But the latter, who
is by nature suspicious, would he have less distrust and the
opinion of deep respect, that discipline requires that he
have for an officer, would it not be altered?

45

The students of the École militaire will eat out of mess-
kits, will be housed in barracks, and will go to take their
dinners in the kitchen.

46

An assembly of men makes no soldiers; exercise,
instruction, and skill give them the character for it.

47

The assembling of forces, activity and the firm resolu-
tion to die with glory. These are the three great principles
of military art that have always rendered fortune favorable
to me in all my operations. Death is nothing; but to live
vanquished and without glory is to die every day.

48

No events that may take place should ever prevent a military man from obeying, and talent in war consists in removing the difficulties that can make an operation difficult and not in making it fail.

49

Military art is an art which has principles that it is never permissible to violate. To change one's line of operation is an operation of genius, to lose it is such a serious operation that it makes criminal the general who makes himself guilty of it.

50

In war, spies, intelligence count for nothing and it would be to risk the lives of men on weak calculations indeed to trust in them.

51

Make known to me the course of public opinion, not by obscure reports, that do not merit, as you know, any confidence, but by general reports in which I can place my faith.

52

Direct to my cabinet all the newspapers and everything
that is published in the [enemy[3]] kingdom. I shall have
an extract made from these and in this way, I shall learn
a great number of details that it could be interesting
for me know.

53

Finally, one must make war, that is to say, to have
news; by means of priests, mayors, heads of convents, the
principal landowners, the mails one will be perfectly well
informed. The reconnaissance carried out each day in
all quarters can furnish three intercepted postal deliveries,
three reports from men arrested, who will be well treated
and released when they have given the desired information.
We shall then see the enemy coming, we shall be able to
assemble all our forces, conceal our movements from
him and fall onto his flanks the moment he contemplates
an offensive project.

54

It is, then, a fact that, when one is not in a desert, and
when one is in a populated country, that, if the general is
not informed about it, it is because he did not take the
appropriate measures to become so. The services that the

inhabitants render to an enemy general are never done by affection, nor even for money, the most concrete things that one obtains are given in order to obtain safeguards and protection, to preserve their goods, their lives, their city, their monastery.

55
One must oblige people to speak.

56
One must be more calm in the direction of military affairs, and before giving credence to reports, one must discuss them. Everything that spies and agents say that they have not seen with their own eyes is nothing, and often, when they have seen it, is no great matter. What I say to you there is useless, since it is only experience that reduces to their just measure those reports that surprise one in the beginning.

57
War is not the police.

58
The art of the police, in order not to punish often, is to punish severely.

59

Not even a hare should cross over the line. The first one who crosses it, have him shot, innocent or guilty. This terror will be salutary. We are ignorant of what the enemy does, it is imperative that he be ignorant of what we do.

60

Events necessarily modify dispositions of troops. Besides, everything depends on seizing the moment.

61

In politics as in war the lost moment never returns.

62

One must not march against an army that is completely intact as one marches against an army that has been beaten.

63

The military system is to oppose force with force and sound policy requires that one put oneself on guard the instant that a force appears to threaten you.

64

The art consists in making things work, even more than in tiring oneself a great deal.

65

Reputation of arms in war is everything and is equivalent to real forces.

66

Alarm beats down the spirits and paralyzes courage.

67

Hardship, blood, death create enthusiasts, martyrs, give birth to courageous and desperate resolutions.

68

Any troop that is not organized is destroyed when one marches against it.

69

What are the conditions for superiority in an army? 1st its organization; 2nd the habit of war in officer and in soldier; 3rd the confidence of all in themselves; that is to say, bravura, patience and everything that the idea of self gives in the way of moral resources.

70

One of the first principles of war is to exaggerate one's forces and not to diminish them.

NOTES

1. It is known that Napoleon never wrote the treatise on war which he projected. And, it is in bringing together whatever, in his conversations, letters, proclamations and directives, was related to it that an individual might attempt to fill such an absence. However, it was necessary to wait until the end of the 19th century for a systematic compilation of diverse sources, classified according to military usage, to be made accessible. Thus, between 1897 and 1901, the publishing house of Baudoin published, in installments, the collection of *Maximes napoléoniennes*, which, with the collaboration of the École de Guerre, General Grisot had brought into good order. In any case, when Major Thomas R. Phillips composed on behalf of the American Army *Roots of Strategy* (Harrisburg, Pennsylvania, 1940), he would refer rather than to the *Maximes* of Napoleon, to an edition of 1827, the first of its kind, so it seems, and very incomplete since it took account of only seventy-eight maxims (Editions Anselin). On the other hand, on behalf of the Club de l'honnête homme, General Gallois would take up again in 1965 an identical principle of presentation *grosso modo* to that of Grisot. Consequently, we could only choose another order, in order that the text be read *actively*. (Y.C.)

2. In italics in a text on the necessity of the offensive in Italy. (Y.C.)

3. Original editor's note. (Y.C.)

II. Defensive

It is in ordinary times and
during peace that one must show
wisdom and foresight.

1

The art of being sometimes very bold and sometimes very prudent is the art of success.

2

The records of the dispositions of armies are for me the most agreeable books of literature in my library, and those that I read with the greatest pleasure in my moments of leisure.

3

A head without a memory is a fort without a garrison.

4

Military men are strongly divided on the question of whether there are greater advantages in making or in defending against an attack, but there is no doubt at all about this question, when, on one side there are battle-hardened troops, skilled in maneuver, having little artillery, and on the other there is a much larger army, having in its train a great deal of artillery, but whose officers and soldiers are little hardened to battle.

5

It is by vigor and energy that one saves one's troops, that one acquires their esteem and one compels submission from the ill-natured ones.

6

When you are driven from an initial position, you must reassemble your columns far enough to the rear that the enemy cannot hinder them, for the most troublesome thing that can happen to you is for your columns to be attacked in isolation before their assembling.

7

One must always make one's retreat towards one's reinforcements.

8

Never place between the various corps of your battle line any interval through which the enemy might penetrate.

9

In the defensive order, one must assemble one's troops, keep them on a battle footing before daylight until the return of the reconnaissance parties that one has sent out towards every position.

10

In guarding a defensive line, the general must have clearly foreseen everything that the enemy might do according to all hypotheses. The enemy can present itself at three or four points. It is imperative, in all these hypotheses, that there be no great time lost in deliberations; that one be able to ploy from right to left or from left to the right without making sacrifices, for, in combined maneuvers, the hesitations of irresolution, which are born of the contradictory pieces of news that follow rapidly one upon the other, lead to misfortunes.

11

If you never depart from the principle that the enemy will never attack directly any point which has no objective—if you guard all points—you will succeed at nothing.

12

The mania for guarding all points in a difficult moment exposes one to great misfortunes.

13

The seizing of a convoy, the surprising of a magazine
give the advantage to a very much inferior army, without
either measuring its strength or running any risks,
in the attempt to lift a siege or to cause the failure of an
operation.

14

Fortresses are useful in defensive war as in offensive
war; there is no doubt that they cannot alone take the
place of an army, but they are the only means that one
may have to retard, to hobble, to weaken, to disquiet
a victorious enemy.

15

I would ask if it were possible to plan a war without
fortresses, and I declare that it is not. Without depot forts,
one cannot establish good campaign plans, and without
what I would call campaign forts, that is to say as shelter
from hussars and partisans, one cannot make an offensive
war. Thus, several generals who, in their wisdom, rejected
fortresses, ended by concluding that one could not make
a war of invasion. But how many fortresses are required?
It is here that one will become convinced that it is
with fortresses as it is with the placement of troops.

Would you pretend to defend an entire frontier with a cordon? You are weak everywhere, for finally what is human is limited: artillery, money, good officers, good generals, none of that is infinite, and if you are obliged to remain weak everywhere, you are strong nowhere.

The forts of certain great cities, of principal ports and of islands can have some importance, but this importance is secondary. Forts that defend defiles or mountain passes can be useful, but their utility is secondary.

Both are campaign forts, though permanent fortifications: I call them this because they can serve to shelter a detachment, a battalion, whether against a debarkation, or against an invasion, when the French army while superior should at the time find itself momentarily inferior at the point of the debarkation or of invasion. Before the great superiority of the enemy might be well established, these forts could be of service and aid the defensive maneuvers of the French army, but they will fall the moment the superiority of the enemy over the French army should become well established. It is impossible that an army two or three times stronger not obtain a decisive advantage over the French army. But must six thousand, eight thousand or twelve thousand men, that events of general policy may cause to be placed in a country, be destroyed and without resources after a few engagements? Must the

munitions, hospitals and magazines dispersed at random
fall and become the prey of the enemy the moment it
should gain superiority in the campaign over my army?
No! That is what must be foreseen and avoided. One can
only accomplish this through the establishment of a great
depot fort, which would serve as the redoubt of all
defense, which would contain all the hospitals, the magazines, the establishments where all troops would come to
regroup, to reassemble, whether to withdraw therein, or
to take the field, if such be the nature of the events and of
the strength of the enemy army. This is the so called
central fort. As long as it exists, they may have lost some
engagements, but suffered only the ordinary losses of war;
as long as it exists, they may, after having caught their
breath and taken some repose, return to seize the victory,
or at least to offer these two advantages: of occupying a
number three times their size in the siege of this fort, and
of giving three or four months time for the arrival of their
relief; for as long as the fort is not taken, the fate of the
province is not decided and the immense materiel
attached to the defense of such a large province is not lost.

Once a central fort comes into existence, all campaign
plans of the generals must be made in relation to it! Once
a superior army has debarked in a port of any kind or
attacks a frontier, the attention of the generals must be to

direct all operations in such a manner that their retreat to the central fort be always assured. They must see the province in the central fort.

16

Depot forts must be studied by the engineering corps, the artillery corps and the quartermaster corps from two points of view: the one, from the point of view of the defense proper of the fort, and the other, as the depot of the army and often the pivot of maneuvers of the army.

17

My opinion is that an earthwork sometimes has advantages over a masonwork because cannonballs bury themselves in it; but the advantage of masonry is to permit a savings in the garrison that guards a fort.

18

In the forts, I want no building that can be burnt. Forts are encumbered by buildings that three artillery shells could set ablaze; after which one must give them up. A long period of peace has introduced this abuse. I prefer to house troops in wooden barracks to be demolished in case of attack.

19

With mediocre troops one must turn up a great deal of earth.

20

One does not even have an army, if one cannot entrench oneself.

21

It is a bad course of action to allow oneself to become shut up in an entrenched camp.

22

Modern generals have renounced the system of entrenched camps in order to supplant it with that of well chosen natural positions.

23

One must never think of any sort of siege before there has even been a battle.

24

Infernal machines, even bombardments, are counted as nothing in time of war. Bombs do nothing to ramparts, trenches, counterscarps; bombs are useful as a combined means of an orderly siege.

25

A post is only a machine of war which should always play its role.

26

To be honorable, a capitulation must stipulate difficult conditions for the garrison. There is always a presumption against a garrison who takes leave of a fort over a bridge of gold.

27

A fort must be defended until there is neither bread nor munitions, or else until the enemy, having crossed the trench, has lodged in the breach; still the commanding officer is at fault who has not established a retrenchment to render the breach useless.

28

When armies believe it possible to leave a critical position by means of an agreement without dishonoring themselves, all is lost. It would be just as good to confide the defense and the honor of arms to old women armed with their spindles.

29

The keys to a fortress are well worth the freedom of its garrison, when it has resolved not to leave it except in freedom.

30

Forbid holding parleys; they are only a means that our enemies have always made use of against us.

31

When an army has experienced defeats, the manner of assembling its detachments or its relief troops is the most delicate operation of war, the one that requires most of all, on the part of the general, the deep knowledge of the principles of the art; it is then above all that their violation brings a defeat and produces a catastrophe.

32

Half of the art of war consists in the art of rapidly regrouping one's army, of sparing useless movements and, as a consequence, the health of the soldier.

33

All the small offensive operations that an army on the defensive can carry out prepare for those that will take place upon the arrival of relief troops and give the army the sphere of confidence and of activity that it should have. At the same time, they procure the means of gathering news and of preventing the kind of news that spreads in camps and that tends to discourage the soldier and to give rise to insolence among the inhabitants.

34

You must proceed from a defensive order that is so redoubtable, that the enemy does not dare attack you and abandon any position behind you, except the defensive positions for your capital, in order to completely assume the offensive against the enemy who, once the incursion has been made, should be able to attempt nothing. That is the art of war. You will see many people who fight well and none who knows the application of this principle.

35

The entire art of war consists of a well reasoned, extremely circumspect defense, and of an audacious and rapid offense.

III. Offensive

When one knows the objective towards
which one must advance, with a little
reflection, the means come easily.

1

One does great things only insofar as one knows how to concentrate oneself entirely on an object and to advance through reversals towards a single objective.

2

The passage from the defensive order to the offensive order is one of the most delicate operations of war.

3

One must not, above all, leave the defensive line on which troops recuperate and rest, without having a definite project, that leaves no uncertainty as to the operations to follow. It would be a great misfortune to leave this line only to be subsequently obliged to take it up again. In war, three quarters of things are moral affairs, the balance of forces is but the other quarter.

4

In mountain warfare, the one who attacks has a disadvantage; even in offensive war, the art consists in having only defensive engagements and in obliging the enemy to attack.

5

The first condition for a field of battle is to not have defiles at one's rear.

6

Conserve with care and never abandon lightheartedly your line of operations.

7

A good infantry is without a doubt the principal strength of the army, but if it must fight against a greatly superior artillery, it will become demoralized and will be destroyed.

8

The campaign is going to exhaust a great number of officers; one must therefore have some on hand to replace them, without making too rapid advancements, which would not attain the objective. If you have need of officers, and non-commissioned officers, the Army of Spain is an inexhaustible source; I authorize you to summon them.

9

It is from thirty to fifty years of age that a man is in possession of his full powers; it is thus the most favorable age for war.

10

The levies of volunteers and other measures of this nature expend money and give no result. Make certain that conscripts are well drilled and that your supply depots are well maintained.

11

Give yourself every chance of success when you plan to engage in battle, above all if you are to oppose a great captain, for if you are beaten, though you were in the center of your magazines, near to your forts, woe to the vanquished.

12

You have taken the elite companies of the cavalry to form your guard, so that these regiments no longer have any strength and no longer render any service whatsoever. Isolating a small number of men is the art of making useless a great number.

13

In having a guard of six thousand men and in giving them such considerable pay, I had as my objective giving recompense to the army; if not for this consideration of giving recompense to the army, I would have had but four hundred men of the guard, or at least I would have had some regiments that were a bit better looked after than the others, but who would not have been paid any more.

14

In war it is shoes that are always lacking.

15

The drum imitates the noise of the cannon; it is the best of all the instruments: it never explodes and never goes out of tune.

16

It is fire, that is the principal means of the moderns.

17

It is a principle of war that when one can make use of thunder, one must prefer it to the cannon.

18

Cannons, like all other arms, must be grouped together, if one wishes to obtain a significant result.

19

One fights with cannons as one fights with one's fists.

20

Whatever one may say to you, never believe that one fights with cannons as one fights with one's fists. Once firing has commenced, the least shortage of munitions during the action renders useless whatever one had done at the beginning.

21

An artillery officer who runs short of munitions in the middle of a battle deserves death.

22

An artillery commander who sends out faulty munitions, according to military law, deserves death.

23

I have accustomed the officers who serve under me to granting favors, not to receiving them.

24

An order must always be executed. When it is not, a crime takes place, and the guilty must be punished.

25

An army that would paralyze, for the entire duration of a battle, half of its artillery and all of its heavy cavalry, would be nearly certain to be beaten.

26

The musket is the best engine of war ever invented by men.

27

It is not necessary to teach soldiers to run, to jump, to hide behind trees, but one must accustom them, when they are cut off from their leaders, to preserve their sang-froid, and to not allow themselves to be overcome by needless terror.

28

Discipline binds troops to their colors; it is not harangues at the moment of battle that makes them brave: the old soldiers listen little, the young soldiers forget at the first cannon shot. If harangues, reasoned arguments

are useful, it is during the course of a campaign: for
destroying insinuations, false rumors, maintaining a good
opinion in camp, furnishing the material for conversations
in bivouacs.

29

If, for fear of being defeated, one did not turn to the
army, it would be useless to raise armies.

30

As for moral courage, that of two o'clock in the
morning is extremely rare; that is to say, the spontaneous
courage that, in spite of the most sudden events,
nonetheless leaves intact freedom of mind, of judgment
and of decision.

31

In all battles, a moment always arrives when the
bravest soldiers after having made the greatest efforts feel
themselves disposed to flight. This terror comes from a
lack of confidence in their courage; it takes only a trivial
incident, a pretext to give them back this courage: the
great art is of giving birth to these.

32

War is a serious game in which one can compromise one's reputation and one's country; to be reasonable about it, one must feel and know in one's bones whether or not one is made for this profession.

33

It is the totality of maneuvers, of the training of officers, that constitutes a true army, it is also what shelters civilized Europe from the ignorance and from the ferocious courage of the barbarians.

34

One must never leave the enemy any advantage, even of opinion, and the soldier is always struck when he sees that the arms of the enemy, especially if from a distance, shoot farther than his own.

35

A campaign plan must have foreseen everything that the enemy can do, and contain within it the means of undoing it.

36

Military men will not for a long time possess the means of learning to profit from the mistakes that caused the reversals and to appreciate the placements of troops that would have prevented them. The entire War of the Revolution could be fertile with lessons and, in order to gather them up, one must often in vain make long application and long research. This does not come from the facts not having been written down in detail, but from no one concerning themselves with making their reading easy and with giving them the necessary direction to do it with discernment.

37

I have studied history a great deal and often, for lack of a guide, I have been led to lose considerable time in useless reading. I have brought enough interest to geography to recognize that in Paris there cannot be found a single man who keeps completely informed about the discoveries that are made each day and about the changes that endlessly supervene.

38

In the matter of maps, one needs only good ones, or at least one must color the doubtful or bad parts to indicate that one may not trust them.

39

Study the country; local knowledge is a specialized knowledge that one will come up against sooner or later.

40

Experience proves that the greatest failure in general administration is to want to do too much; this leads to not having what one needs.

41

One needs only a single army, for unity of command is of the first necessity in war; one must keep the army assembled, concentrate the greatest possible number of forces on the field of battle, profit by all opportunities; for fortune is a woman, if you miss her today, don't expect to find her tomorrow.

42

The task that the commander of an army has to fulfill is more difficult in modern armies than it was in ancient armies. It is true that his influence is greater on the outcome of battles.

43

A general-in-chief is not protected by the order of a minister or of a prince distant from the field of operations and knowing poorly, or not knowing the latest state of things. 1st Any general-in-chief who undertakes to execute a plan that he finds to be bad and disastrous is a criminal; he must represent, insist that it be changed, finally give his resignation rather than be the instrument of the ruin of his men; 2nd Any general who, in consequence of superior orders, engages in a battle, having the certainty of losing it, is a criminal; 3rd A general-in-chief is the first officer of the military hierarchy. The minister, the prince give instructions to which he should conform himself in soul and conscience, but these instructions are never military orders and do not require a passive obedience; 4th A military order itself does not require a passive obedience except when it is given by a superior, who, being present at the moment he gives it, has a knowledge of the state of things, can listen to the objections and give explanations to the one who should execute the order.

44

The direction of military affairs is only half the work of a general; to establish and to secure his communications is one of the most important objectives. Secure your communications very quickly indeed.

45

Such are the drawbacks of the law that would have it that commissioners of war be only civil agents, while they are in need of greater courage and military habits than the officers themselves. The courage that is necessary for them should be all of the moral order; it is never the fruit of the habit of danger.

46

It is not the troops who fail you, it is the manner of assembling them and of acting with vigor.

47

The corps of the enemy can be destroyed by combined maneuvers, but for that, one must make a decision on the spur of the moment, have one's army at hand and have the knowledge of one's art. If one obtains a decisive victory against all his assembled forces, or several victories against his isolated corps, these victories must counsel the decision to be made. But all these engagements must be made following the rules of war, that is to say having one's line of communications secured.

48

One must not come to bear at all the points of the circumference when one does not have open communications, rather one must form a single huge mass against the enemy, give him no breathing space so that he will fall into disarray.

49

One must have made war for a long time in order to conceive the value as a threat of a position held in force and offensively; one must have undertaken a great number of offensive operations to know how the least event or sign encourages or discourages, decides one operation or another.

50

In war, one sees one's own ills and not those of the enemy; one must show confidence.

51

All war must be methodical, because all war must be conducted in conformity with the principles and rules of the art and with an objective; it must be pursued with forces proportionate to the obstacles that one foresees.

52

The loss of time is irreparable in war; the reasons that one may allege are all bad, for operations fail only through delays.

53

The only loss that you cannot repair is the dead.

54

An army that marches in conquest of a country has its wings supported by neutral countries or by great natural obstacles, be it by great rivers, or by ranges of mountains; or it has only one of them, or none so supported. In the first case, it has only not to allow itself to be penetrated frontally; in the second case, it must support itself on the supported wing; in the third case, it must maintain its corps well supported at the center and never divide itself; for if it is a problem to conquer having one's wings exposed, this inconvenience is double if one has four of them; triple if one has six of them, quadruple if one has eight of them; that is to say if one divides oneself in two, three or four different corps. The line of operations of an army, in the first case, can support itself on the left side and on the right; in the second case, it should support itself on the supported flank; in the third case, it must be perpendicular to the middle of the line of march of the army. In every case, one must, every five or six marches: have a fortress or an entrenched position on the line of operations in order to assemble magazines of subsistence and of war there, to organize convoys there and to make a center of movement there, a point of reference that shortens the line of operations.

55

Night marches are advantageous above all when one has the country on one's side.

56

Most often, one should have an avant-garde where the general-in-chief should be found, in order to direct the movements of his army from there. For the avant-garde one must have light cavalry, heavy cavalry, some elite corps of infantry and a sufficient quantity of artillery, in order to be able to maneuver, to contain the enemy, to give time to the army to arrive, to baggage vans, to supply vans to move into position.

57

The duty of an avant-garde or of a rear-guard is neither to advance nor retreat, but to maneuver.

58

An untrained troop would be only an object of embarrassment to the avant-garde.

59

A forward movement without strong combinations can succeed when the enemy is in retreat, but it can never succeed when the enemy is in position and has decided to defend itself; then, it is a system or a combination that causes a battle to be won.

60

In war, one makes decisions in the presence of the enemy, one always has night on one's side to prepare. The enemy does not move into position without one's noticing it, but one must not calculate theoretically what one wants to do, since that is subordinated to what the enemy does and will do; according to the laws of war, any general who loses his line of communication deserves death.

61

The professor of philosophy, who, in some great city—I no longer know which one—spoke for a long time in the presence of Hannibal, pretended he was also a great military man. The perfection or the system of modern warfare consists, you pretend, in throwing one corps of the army to the right, one to the left, yielding the center to the enemy, and even of placing oneself behind a line of fortresses. If these principles were taught to youths, they would set back military science four hundred years, and every time that one conducted oneself thus and that one should have affair with an active enemy, who had even the least knowledge of ambushes in war, he would cut off one of your corps and smash the other.

62

There is no natural order of battle. Anything one should prescribe along those lines would be of more harm than use.

63

Success in war depends so much on sweep of
vision and on the moment, that the battle of Austerlitz,
won so promptly would have been lost, had I attacked
six hours earlier.

64

The fate of a battle is the result of an instant, of a
thought; one approaches with diverse combinations, one
becomes involved, one fights a certain length of time,
the decisive moment presents itself, a moral spark makes
its pronouncement and the smallest reserve realizes its
ultimate end.

65

A modern army should, then, avoid being outflanked,
enveloped, encircled; it should occupy a front as extended
as its own line of battle; if it occupied a square surface
and a front insufficient for its deployment, it would be
encircled by an army of equal strength and exposed to all
the fire of its projectile weapons, which would converge
upon it and reach all points of its encampment, without its
being able to answer such a redoubtable fire except with a
portion of its own. In this position, it would be attacked
outrageously, in spite of its entrenchments, by an army of

equal strength, even by an inferior army. The modern encampment can only be defended by the army itself, and in the absence of this latter it can hardly be guarded by a simple detachment.

66

One must engage in battle only when one has no new opportunities for which to hope, since by its nature the fate of a battle is always doubtful, but once it has been resolved upon, one must conquer or perish.

67

When one is within range of striking to the quick, one must not allow oneself to be led astray by contrary maneuvers.

68

It is not by dispersing one's troops and by scattering them that one arrives at a result.

69

It is thus a fundamental principle that an army always maintain its columns assembled, in such a manner that the enemy cannot make its way among them. If for any reason at all, one should depart from this principle,

the detached corps must be independent in their
operations and direct themselves to assemble at a fixed
point, towards which they would march without hesitation
and without new orders, so that they be less exposed
to being attacked in isolation.

70

The rules of war require that in important circumstances such as those, one does not hold to rumors,
but one maneuvers in order to oblige the enemy to show
itself and allow itself to be counted.

71

You will take care to drive out the parties of enemy
infantry on your right by means of your observation corps.

72

One must reconnoiter this entire position and the
advantage one may draw from swamps and from natural
obstacles; it is in this case that any natural obstacle is
good, because it tends to shelter a less numerous corps
from a more numerous corps, and obliges the enemy to
make dispositions which give one the time to act.

73

When the army opposing you is protected by a river
on which it has several bridgeheads, one must not make a
frontal approach; this disposition disperses your army and
exposes it to being cut off. One must approach the stream
that you want to cross in columns in echelon, so that there
is but a single column, the furthest forward, that the
enemy can attack without offering its flank. During this
time, your light troops will mass along the bank, and when
you have fixed upon the point where you wish to cross, a
point which should always be distant from the leading
echelon, in order to better deceive your enemy, you will
proceed there rapidly and throw out your bridge.

74

From a line one can hope only for the following
advantages: to render the position of the enemy so difficult
that he throws himself into false operations and that
he is beaten by inferior forces, or, if, one has at one's head
a general who is prudent and of genius, to oblige him to
cut methodically through obstacles created at leisure and
thereby to gain time; in the contrary case, on the side
of the French army, to aid the weakness of the general,
to render his position so clearly marked and so easy that
he cannot commit great errors and, finally to give him

the time to wait for relief troops. In the art of war, as
in mechanics, time is the great element between weight
and power.

75

If the enemy has taken up a good position and is waiting for you, I recommend you reconnoiter well and well
establish your system before attacking. A forward movement without strong combinations can succeed when the
enemy is in retreat, but it never succeeds when the enemy
is in position and has decided to defend itself; then, it is a
system or a combination that causes a battle to be won.

76

The art today is to attack everything one encounters,
in order to beat the enemy in detail and while he
assembles. When I say that one must attack everything
that one encounters, I mean that one must attack everything that is in movement and not in a position that
renders it too much superior.

77

In so difficult an art as war, it is often in the system
for a campaign that one conceives the system for a battle;
only very experienced military men will understand that.

78

It is a fundamental principle to make no detachment on the eve of an attack, because, during the night, the state of things can change, be it by movements of retreat by the enemy, or by the arrival of great reinforcements that place him in the position of taking the offensive and render fatal the premature dispositions that you have made. One is often deceived in war concerning the strength of the enemy with whom one must enter into combat. Prisoners know only their corps, commanders make quite unreliable reports; this has brought about the adoption of one axiom that remedies all: that an army should every day, every night, every hour, be ready to offer all the resistance of which it is capable.

79

A line of operations should never pass through a mountainous country: 1st because one cannot live there; 2nd because one encounters there, at every step, defiles that one would have to occupy by means of fortresses; 3rd because marching there is difficult and slow; 4th because columns of regular troops can be stopped by ragged peasants leaving the plow and be defeated and undone; 5th because the spirit of mountain warfare is to never attack; even when one wishes to conquer, one must set out

by maneuvers of position, that leave no other alternative
to the corps charged with the defense but to itself attack or
to retreat; 6th finally, because a line of operations should
serve for retreat; and how can one imagine retreating
through gorges, defiles, precipices?

80

An army disposed in two or three bivouac lines
allows only a single mass of smoke to be perceived which
the enemy will confound with atmospheric fog. It is
impossible to count the number of fires; it is very easy
to count the number of tents and to sketch out the
positions that they occupy.

81

It is necessary to classify the objectives to pursue
according to their importance and to form a clear idea of
them for oneself.

82

Tentative gestures, mezzo-termine ruin everything
in war.

83

The principles of Caesar were the same as those of
Hannibal: to keep his forces assembled, to be vulnerable
at no point, to move with speed to important points, to
make use of moral resources, of the reputation of his arms,
of the fear that he inspired as well as of political means
to maintain the fidelity of his allies, and the obedience of
conquered peoples.

84

Every offensive war is a war of invasion; every well-
conducted war is a methodical war. Defensive war does
not exclude attack, just as offensive war does not exclude
defense, though its objective be of crossing the frontier
and invading the enemy country. The principles of war are
those that have directed the great captains whose lofty
deeds history has transmitted to us: Alexander, Hannibal,
Caesar, Gustavus-Adolphus, Turenne, Prince Eugène,
Frederick the Great. The history, made with care of the
eighty-four campaigns of these great men would be a
complete treatise on the art of war; the principles that one
must follow in defensive and offensive war would flow
from them as from a spring.

85

The character of our nation is to be far too lively in prosperity. If we take as a basis of all operations true politics, which is nothing but the calculation of combinations and of odds, we will be for a long time the great nation and the arbiter of Europe. I say further: we hold the balance of Europe; we shall make it incline as we wish and, if such be the order of destiny, I see no impossibility in our achieving within a few years even those great results that the heated and enthusiastic imagination half-glimpses, and that the man who is extremely cold, constant and rational, will alone attain.

86

The Frenchman has distinguished himself at all times by this spirit of opposition that has become more pronounced today, now that war and revolution have exalted character.

87

With weakness one does not govern peoples and one draws misfortunes upon them; I am indeed fearful that you should display more of it than what your character is susceptible to. Did you hope to govern peoples without at first making them unhappy? You know quite well that in the matter of government, justice means force as virtue.

88

The praises of enemies are suspect, they can only flatter a man of honor when they are given after the cessation of hostilities.

89

A bit of address, of dexterity, the ascendancy that I have gained, some severe examples alone give to these peoples a great respect for the nation and an interest, though it be extremely weak, in the cause that we defend.

90

Pillage annihilates everything, even the army that practices it.

91

Advise the soldiers to spare the country; in ruining it, we deprive ourselves of resources.

92

In all countries, by holding the principal cities or positions, one may control them easily, by having under one's hand the bishops, the magistrates, the principal landowners, who are interested in maintaining order under their responsibility.

93

There are in the *Rêveries* of the Maréchal de Saxe, among many excessively mediocre things, some ideas on the manner of making enemy countries render tribute without exhausting the army, which struck me as good. Put their contents in an instructional manual to be sent to the regiments of Spain.

94

The policy that you are following with the people of Naples is the inverse of the policy to follow with conquered peoples. March in force, do not disperse your troops. What is the meaning of this national guard of Naples? This is to rely upon a reed for your support, if not to give an army to your enemy. Oh! how little you know men!

95

The events of war sometimes bring along in their wake measures of strictness and even of violence, that it is impossible for sovereign authority to foresee and to prevent.

96

As long as you have made no examples you will not be master. To any conquered people a revolt is necessary, and I would regard a revolt as the father of a family sees smallpox in his children: provided it does not weaken the patient too much, it is a healthy crisis.

97

Conquered provinces must be held in obedience to the conqueror through moral resources, the account-ability of the communes, the mode of organization of the administrations; hostages are among the most powerful means; but, for that, it is necessary that they be numerous and chosen from among the most influential men and that the people can be persuaded that the death of the hostages will be the immediate consequence of the violation of their allegiance.

98

In the occupation of a country, the principal points must be occupied, and from there mobile columns must move out to pursue brigands. The experience of the

Vendée has proven that it was best to have mobile columns, spread out and multiplied everywhere, not stationary corps.

99

Conquered peoples become the subjects of the conqueror only by a mixture of politics and severity, and by their intermingling with the army. These things have been lacking in Spain.

100

The conduct of a general in a conquered country is surrounded on all sides by reefs; if he is hard, he irritates and increases the number of his enemies; if he is gentle, he gives rise to hopes that make the abuses and vexations inevitably connected with the state of war stand out even further. However that may be, if a rebellion in these circumstances is calmed in time, and the conqueror knows how to employ a mixture of severity, of justice and of gentleness in so doing, it can only have a good effect: it will have been advantageous and will be a new guarantee for the future.

101

It is not by cajoling peoples that one wins them, and it is not with these measures that you will give yourself the means of according just recompense to your army. The peoples of Italy and, peoples, generally, if they perceive no master, are disposed to rebellion and to mutiny. You must understand clearly that if circumstances did not dictate that you had great military maneuvers to perform, the glory would remain to you of knowing how to feed your army and of drawing from the country you are in resources of all kinds; this makes up a great part of the art of war.

102

The first sentiment of hatred of a nation is of being the enemy of another.

103

Nothing is more salutary than terrible examples timely made.

104

It is in flattering peoples that one abases them.

105

A prince of whom it is said: he is a good man
will never be king. You give the appearance of courting
everyone.

106

Experience has taught me that a great act of strength,
in the circumstances in which you find yourself, was
most humane. Weakness by itself is inhumane. After
having done all that moderation dictates, one must display
some of the energy, without which this moderation is
only weakness.

107

Make examples for discipline. At the slightest insult
by a Prussian city, by a village, burn it: even Berlin itself,
if they behave badly.

108

At the beginning of civil wars, one must keep all
troops assembled, because they become electrified and
gather confidence from the strength of the group; they
become attached to it and remain faithful to it.

109

In civil wars it is not given to everyone to know how to conduct himself; one needs something more than military prudence, one needs wisdom, an understanding of men.

110

In party warfare, one who is vanquished for a day is discouraged for a long time. It is above all in civil wars that fortune is necessary.

111

Machiavelli said in vain, fortresses are not worth the favor of peoples.

Postcards from the Berezina

Keith Sanborn

The Germans are such prudent realists that not one of their wishes and their wildest fancies ever extends beyond the bare actualities of life. And this reality, no more no less, is accepted by those who rule over them. They too are realists, they are utterly removed from all thought and human greatness, they are ordinary officers and provincial Junkers, but they are not mistaken, they are right: just as they are, they are perfectly adequate to the task of exploiting and ruling over this animal kingdom—for here as everywhere rule and exploitation are identical concepts. When they make people pay them homage, when they gaze out over the teeming throng of brainless creatures, what comes into their minds but the thought that occurred to Napoleon on the Berezina. It is said that he pointed to the mass of drowning men and declared to his entourage: Voyez ces crapauds! [Look at those toads!] The story is probably invented, but it is true nevertheless. Despotism's only thought is disdain for mankind, dehumanized man; and it is a thought superior to many others in that it is also a fact. In the eyes of the despot men are always debased. They drown before his eyes and on his behalf in the mire of common life from which, like toads, they always rise up again. If even men capable of great vision, like Napoleon before he succumbed to his dynastic madness, are overwhelmed by this insight, how should a quite ordinary king be an idealist in the midst of such a reality?

Karl Marx
***Letters from the Franco-German Yearbook**, May 1843*

Excursus in the form of a postcard

In the museum of the Château de Rueil-Malmaison there once stood—and may still—what the faded postcard lent to me by a friend identifies in three languages as the "frock coat and hat of the Emperor." The card displays the familiar black shape seen on the emperor's head in endless battle scenes and cognac ads on a sumptuous scarlet ground above a long gray double-breasted coat. The hat recalls the ones worn by Franco's Guardia Civil, except that here it's flipped hiphop back to front. The hat and coat float weightlessly: the stub of the display form pokes through where the emperor's neck once did, never touching the hat, and where the stand should replace the emperor's legs, the coat shows no visible means of support. These flat contradictions of the laws of physics and representation involuntarily recall for me the marvelous illusions of Méliès: a still from some lost version of *The Inn where no man rests*. This paradoxical effect may be the result of some deft erasures, or perhaps only of the mechanical wear of the printing plates, for the card has been run so many times its softened contours give as much the appearance of a drawing as of a photograph.

Kojève, Hegel, and Napoleon

Hegel, from his window at Jena at the moment of Napoleon's triumph on the battlefield nearby, and Alexandre Kojève, from the vantage afforded by the École des Hautes Études over a century later, regarded Napoleon as the last man in History and its greatest—except perhaps for themselves. Both History, so they thought, and men came to an end in Napoleon. Within a few days of completing his *Phenomenology*, Hegel candidly expressed his enthusiasm for Napoleon in a letter to his friend Niethammer:

> I saw the Emperor—that Worldsoul—riding out to reconnoiter the city; it is truly a wonderful sensation to see such an individual, concentrated here on a single point, astride a single horse, yet reaching across the world and ruling it... To make such progress from Thursday to Monday is possible only for this extraordinary man, whom it is impossible not to admire.

Hegel, in realizing Napoleon's importance, thought himself in some measure superior to History and to other men, as the "Sage" who had been conscious of this moment and this man. Napoleon seemed to appear as the inevitable outcome of Hegel's own Philosophy. Kojève, in his *Introduction to the Reading of Hegel*, analyzes the relationship of Hegel to Napoleon by reading it through Hegel's *Phenomenology*:

> ...Now, in fact, what is it to "understand" Napoleon, other than to understand him as the one who perfects the ideal of the French Revolution by realizing it? And can one understand this idea, this Revolution, without understanding the ideology of the Aufklärung, the Enlightenment? Generally speaking, to understand Napoleon is to understand him in relation to the whole of anterior historical evolution, to understand the whole of universal history. Now, almost none of the philosophers contemporary with Hegel posed this problem for himself. And none of them, except Hegel, resolved it. For Hegel is the only one able to accept, and to justify, Napoleon's existence—that is, to "deduce" it from the first principles of his philosophy, his anthropology, his conception of history. The others consider themselves obliged to condemn Napoleon, that is, to condemn the historical reality; and their philosophical systems—by that very fact are all condemned by

that reality.

Is he not this Hegel, a thinker endowed with absolute Knowledge, because on the one hand, he lives in Napoleon's time, and, on the other, is the only one to understand him?

This is precisely what Hegel says in the *Phenomenology.*

Absolute Knowledge became—*objectively*—possible because in and by Napoleon the *real* process of historical evolution, in the course of which man *created* new Worlds and *transformed* himself by creating them, came to its end. To reveal *this* World, therefore, is to reveal *the* World—that is, to reveal being in *the completed* totality of its spatial-temporal existence. And—*subjectively*—absolute Knowledge became possible because a man named Hegel was able to understand the *World* in which he lived and to understand *himself* as living in and understanding this World...

Kojève later extended this extraordinary analytical apparatus to include Marx and finally himself. His ultimate conclusion was that by so deeply probing the depths of Hegel's perfected understanding of History, he had himself, transcended even that analysis to become, in effect, a "god." This had come about because he had achieved his own absolute knowledge of Hegel's absolute knowledge of the world and reached consciousness of Hegel's consciousness of that achievement. As Shadia Drury points out in her pioneering study, *Alexandre Kojève: the roots of postmodern politics*, Kojève at first saw himself as occupying the same position with respect to Stalin that Hegel had occupied with respect to Napoleon. He initially believed that Stalin was simply completing the work begun by Napoleon in establishing the Universal Homogenous State. Though Kojève remained content to admire Stalin at a distance rather than return to the Soviet State he had fled in his youth, he was reported to have been grief-stricken at Stalin's death. Kojève later came to revise his thinking, somewhat. Hegel's analysis by itself had been completely adequate: History had indeed ended in 1806, as Napoleon brought the downfall of Prussia and consolidated his conquests in the form of the Universal Homogeneous Revolutionary State which remained ultimately unsurpassed. This revision, however, seems not to have greatly altered either his admiration for Stalin, nor his sense of the importance of his own work in Philosophy or at the French Foreign Ministry of Economic Affairs, laying the groundwork for the European Union.

Napoleon '06 to Napoleon '68

If Kojève's philosophical analysis seems somewhat grandiose from the vantage of the last years of the 20th century, its ingenuity and vast scope have attracted numerous influential adherents. The consideration of the question of the End of History lies at the center of post-modern political theory. Bataille, Breton, Queneau, Lacan, Merleau-Ponty, even Alan Bloom studied with Kojève. Kojève's influence on Foucault through Bataille was immense as was his influence on Fukuyama through Bloom. And if the importance of Bloom or Fukuyama in intellectual history remains negligible, they have not been without their influence on the tyrants who have contributed to shaping the History they have deduced from the principles expounded by Bloom and Fukuyama. As Shadia Drury points out, the entire lot are indebted to Kojève's reading of Hegel through Nietzsche, Heidigger, and Marx, though each recasts Hegel in his own image.

It is this same imaginative synthesis of German intellectual history—with Reich's more materialist account of consciousness significantly displacing Heidigger's—that formed the theoretical basis for the radical political developments of the 1960s in France, including that of the Situationist

International. The following passage, from a section Bloom chose not to include in his English language edition of Kojève's *Introduction to the Reading of Hegel*, suggestively links Hegel with Napoleon *and* the worker-soldiers of the French Revolution:

> …the final goal of human becoming is, according to Hegel, the synthesis of the warlike existence of the Master and the life of labor of the Slave. The Man who is fully satisfied by his existence, and who achieves precisely thereby the historical evolution of humanity, is the Citizen of the universal and homogenous State, that is, for Hegel, the worker-soldier of the revolutionary armies of Napoleon. Therefore it is indeed war (for Recognition) that terminates History and carries Man to his perfection (=satisfaction). Thus, Man can perfect himself only to the extent that he is mortal and accepts, with an awareness of what is involved, the risk of life.

Political agency oscillates between the existential struggle of each individual and his political abstraction at the hands of great men—whether Emperor General or Bureaucrat Philosopher. While Kojève is a perfect anti-Situationist in his ultimate appeal to statist values, he held in common

with the Situationists the recognition of the critical impor-
tance of Hegel and Nietzsche in reading Marx and of the
fundamental comparability of East Block Bureaucratic
State Capitalism (Debord's *concentrated spectacle*) and
Western Democratic Capitalism (Debord's *diffuse spectacle*).
The Situationists stood in radical opposition to Kojève,
however, in believing neither in the finality of the End of
History as Hegel saw it, nor in reconciliation with the
Homogenous Universal State as its dutiful citizens.

Debord articulates the Situationist critique of Hegel in
Section 76 of his book *Society of the Spectacle*; in the film
he based on this book, Debord uses the following excerpt
in a voice-over accompanying an image of Hegel:

> The paradox which consists in suspending the
> meaning of all reality in favor of its historical
> accomplishment, and in revealing this meaning at
> the same time by constituting itself as the accom-
> plishment of history, devolves from the simple fact
> that the thinker of the bourgeois revolutions of the
> 17th and 18th centuries sought in his philosophy
> only reconciliation with their result.

Both Kojève and the Situationists understood the critical

importance of Hegelian and Marxian dialectics but they understood the dual sense of *Aufhebung*—transcendence and cancellation—from opposing points of view. Kojève worked for the creation of a hierarchical, technocratic, pan-European apotheosis of the State to surpass the European Nation State by bringing its various forms into conformity and subjection. The Situationists dedicated themselves to surpassing the Nation State by working to destroy it in all its forms and to abolish class society, to make possible a decentralized network of Workers' Councils, "or something like them." While the Situationists never ultimately resolved in practice the question of organization, theirs was a productive negativity. It is neither ironic nor coincidental that Kojève exited the stage of world history in Brussels in May of 1968 at the precise moment the SI effectively surpassed itself as a revolutionary organization by joining the Occupations movement in Paris.

The Maastricht treaty and the disappearance of the Berlin Wall may both be read as footnotes to Kojève. In this light, each testifies as much to the continuing attraction as to the transcendence of necrophiliac stalinism; the fetishism of Napoleonic imperial regalia persists. Debord saw this dialectical supercession of the opposition of concentrated and diffuse spectacle as yielding a new form he called the *integrated spectacle*. Here, certain structures in opposition disappear, but the stratifications and antagonisms integral to both are preserved as features of the landscape.

Bataille, Nietzsche, Napoleon, Laughter

For Bataille, writing at the eclipse of Surrealism and the ascendancy of Stalinism, Napoleon's recuperation of the French Revolution is emblematic of the fate of utopian idealism:

> Revolutionary idealism tends to make of the revolution an eagle above eagles, a supereagle striking down authoritarian imperialism, an idea as radiant as an adolescent eloquently seizing power for the benefit of utopian enlightenment. This detour naturally leads to the failure of the revolution and, with the help of military fascism, the satisfaction of the elevated need for idealism. The Napoleonic epic represents its least ridiculous development: the castration of an Icarian revolution, shameless imperialism exploiting the revolutionary urge.

In a few short years, Bataille and his European contemporaries would experience the most tragic and shameful developments of their part of this century, as the suppression of Kronstadt became the road to the Moscow purges and the losses at Jarama the road to the genocide of Auschwitz.

Nietzsche—whose philosophizing with a hammer was to deeply mark Bataille's sense of epistemological paradox—had seen Napoleon as a counterpoise to the European herdmen of his century:

> ...the appearance of one who commands unconditionally strikes these herd-animal Europeans as an immense comfort and salvation from a gradually intolerable pressure, as was last attested in a major way by the effect of Napoleon's appearance. The history of Napoleon's reception is almost the history of the higher happiness attained by this whole century in its most valuable human beings and moments.

If Nietzsche held in admiration Napoleon's personal, historical singularity, his qualifying "almost" sounds out the true object of his attention: a chasm of irony opens in the din of this reception, releasing waves of scornful laughter against the masses and their bovine contentment with the loss of individuality and agency. The history of Napoleon's reception in *this* century remains an index to its politics. Though he has remained for many a simple authoritarian or military fetish, I would argue that his potential importance for the latter half of this century would be better gauged by examining the interest devoted to the Emperor General's critique of ideology and to his strategic mastery of the art of war by the Situationist International—and in particular by Debord. For it was the Situationist International, during the tenure of President General de Gaulle, who critiqued most thoroughly not only the capitalism of post-war abundance but Stalinism in all its forms. The hysterical Nietzschean laughter which resounds bitterly through Bataille echoes sharply across the Paris of the Situationists. Bataille's *potlatch* economics, his exploration of sexual and alcoholic excess drive the radical subjectivity which makes possible the Situationist transvaluation of values, synthesizing Nietzsche, Marx and Reich.

The Situationist International is dead!
Long live the Situationist International!

From the early 1970s to the early 1990s, Éditions Champ Libre was the principal publisher of Situationist theory in France. Its catalogues read as maps of Situationist intellectual history. In 1971, Champ Libre published their first edition of Debord's *Society of the Spectacle*. In 1972, Champ Libre published Debord and Sanguinetti's *The True Split in the International*, theorizing the demise of the Situationist International, and Raspaud and Voyer's celebrated reference work on the Situationist International including a list of participants, a chronology, and bibliography "with a list of names insulted." Over the next two decades Champ Libre would publish the collected issues of the *Situationist International* journal, Sanguinetti's deadpan *True Report on the Last Chance of Saving Capitalism in Italy*, and the vast majority of Debord's output, including his *Complete Cinematographic Works*, *Preface to the Fourth Italian Edition of the Society of the Spectacle*, *Commentaries on the Society of the Spectacle*, *Considerations on the Assassination of Gérard Lebovici*, and the first volume of his autobiography, *Panegyric*.

1973 was a particularly busy year in the circles around Champ Libre. With the backing of Gérard Lebovici, the owner of Champ Libre, Debord made the film *Society of the Spectacle* based on his book. Champ Libre also brought into print a number of titles, including two by von Clausewitz (*The Campaign of 1814* and *The Campaign of 1815 in France*) and a collection of Napoleon's remarks on military strategy under the title *How to Make War* [*Comment faire la guerre*]. That edition of Napoleonic maxims was meant, according to its editor, Yann Cloarec, to serve "as a guide for those men and women whose ambition it is to accomplish revolution: to import dialectically the principles of a war among States" to the war between classes.

Since *How to Make War* appeared only after the dissolution of the Situationist International and its editor was never a member of the SI, there is no question of establishing for this edition of Napoleonic maxims a Situationist imprimatur—a hagiographic exercise at best. There are, however, at least two important links between Napoleonic and Situationist understandings of the relations of theory and practice. And it is ultimately that relationship of theory and practice which may establish an index to the politics of this century. The first link is that the critique of *idéologie*—the so-called science of ideas—begun by Napoleon, was carried forward by the Situationists in their attack on the ideological ossifications of institutional Marxism. The second is that Debord, one of the principal theorists of the Situationist International, had a profound interest in military history, the art of war, and in particular in von Clausewitz, who remains by far the most astute and influential analyst of Napoleon.

In any case, it is on that 1973 edition of *How to Make War* published by Champ Libre that the current translation is based. It was chosen first, because, as its editor points out, it is the most extensive collection ever assembled of Napoleonic maxims on the art of war, classified according to military usage. Second, because these texts are arranged according to a dialectical strategy which reveals Napoleon's capacity for adapting the observations of theory to the constantly changing, complex and contradictory conditions of praxis. And finally, because of the light it may reflect not only onto the hysterical historical battles now raging around the Situationist International, but onto the current state of the world and onto practical strategies for changing it. For with the collapse of the Soviet Block and the dawning of the millennium, Kojèvian epigones have once again proclaimed the End of History. The supercession of the dialectic of concentrated and diffuse in the integrated spectacle has created a profound theoretical crisis: received ethical binarisms have collapsed in the bravely virtual new old world, the seemingly seamlessly monolithic digital domain of invisible and environmental binarism.

Ideology and its discontents

Napoleon's critique of ideology began during the Directory shortly after the promulgation of ideology as a self-conscious project. "Idéologie" was the creation of the self-proclaimed "idéologistes," a coterie of savants centered around Destutt de Tracy, who enjoyed state support for their research on projects of scientific governance. Though Napoleon initially cultivated them because of his own interest in scientific governance and because of their position of political and intellectual influence, he soon came to detest them and to detest in particular Destutt de Tracy's invented science of ideas, "idéologie." As Yann Cloarec points out, in his original introduction to this collection of Napoleonic maxims, Napoleon invented the term "idéologue," in order to mock them. Though Napoleon enjoyed moving through the highest intellectual circles of his time, his sense of the limits of the intellect when detached from the experience of everyday life was acute:

> The professor of philosophy, who, in some great city—I no longer know which one—spoke for a long time in the presence of Hannibal, pretended he was also a great military man. The perfection or the system of modern warfare consists, you pretend, in

throwing one corps of the army to the right, one to the left, yielding the center to the enemy, and even of placing oneself behind a line of fortresses. If these principles were taught to youths, they would set back military science four hundred years, and every time that one conducted oneself thus and that one should have affair with an active enemy, who had even the least knowledge of ambushes in war, he would cut off one of your corps and smash the other.

Napoleon summarizes the relationship between the art of war and ideology this way: "The art of war is a simple art and all in the execution; there is nothing vague in it, everything in it is common sense, nothing in it is ideology." Napoleon's ultimate critique of the idéologistes was to sweep them out of power by reorganizing the Institut National. The force of this insight and the fate of these first ideologues seems to have been lost on the technologues of our own era, both within the military and outside it. Debord's observation that, "Revolutionary theory is the enemy of revolutionary ideology and knows that" is the Situationist corollary.

Grounded in this insight, the Situationists developed their principal strategy for warfare on existing conditions, *détournement*:

Short for: detournment of preexisting aesthetic elements. The integration of present or past artistic production into a superior construction of a milieu. In this sense there can be no Situationist painting or music, but only a Situationist use of these means. In a more primitive sense, detournment within the old cultural spheres is a method of propaganda, a method which testifies to the wearing out and loss of importance of those spheres.

The word "détournement" carries with it the charge of a variety of striking associations from hijacking to embezzlement to the seduction of a minor. As a tactic, the Situationist practice of detournment usually took the form of critical recontextualization of images from the mass-media through the addition or alteration of textual elements. Advertisements, cartoons, and films were favored targets and vehicles for this strategy. A prime example is René Viénet's detournment of Do Kwang Gee's Kung-fu film, *The Crush*, to create *Can Dialectics break bricks?* Though recutting of the film seems to play some part, Viénet's main tactic was to add provocative and critical French subtitles to the Chinese language version of the film, which, needless to say, have little or nothing to do with the original dialogue. By this means, an historical struggle by

Korean resistance fighters against a Japanese occupation force is recast as the uprising of anarchist revolutionaries against the bureaucrats in a country "where the ideology is particularly cold." The multi-dimensional topos developed by Viénet directs a trenchant critique at the bureaucrats of the Korean as well as the Chinese and French Communist parties. In 1973, shortly after the appearance of this subtitled version, a second version of *Can Dialectics break bricks?* was created where the Chinese dialogue of the original was removed and the French text of the subtitles of the previous version became spoken dialogue and voice-overs. In this dubbed version, the Party Chairman of the "bureaucrats" sits in his bath, while two young women clad only in short towels soap him down. His First Secretary stands stiffly at attention nearby:

Chairman:

—Ideology reenforces itself as it becomes more atomized. Revolutionary theory transforms itself. It seems their latest discovery is to detourn the mass-media. These detournments disturb me.

First Secretary:

—That, old man, is the beginning of the end. What disturbs me most in this practice is that they are

quite capable of reducing our own wooden language
to shavings if not to sawdust.

Chairman:

—We've got to watch that.

The Situationists read Napoleon as they did Machiavelli:
as a disabused realist who understood the difference
between official pronouncements and the mechanisms of
state power. While opposing the hierarchical imposition of
personal power typified by Napoleon, they shared with
Napoleon a radical subjectivity which held in contempt
the mystifications of ideologues wielding power "in the
name of the people."

The Stage of World History

If Napoleon scorned the scientistic pretensions of the ide-
ologists, he was far from disinterested in social engineering. He aggressively propagandized the conquered peoples of Northern Italy, Southern Germany, and even Egypt.
In Europe he was lionized, at least for a time, by a broad
spectrum of influential intellectuals. In Egypt, Napoleon
made use of French Orientalists to manage the subject
population through local religious leaders. For the dura-

tion of the French occupation this strategy effectively maintained civil order in Cairo. Napoleon's efforts, however, were not only fairly short-lived, they were met with razor-edged critique by the Egyptian chronicler of the French invasion, Al-Jabarti. Al-Jabarti was appalled at French manners—relieving themselves in public, for example—and at the preposterous French religious arguments that Napoleon was a true Muslim because—for among other reasons—he was an enemy of the Pope. Al-Jabarti meticulously dissects the bombastic Arabic proclamations of the French, heaping scorn upon their pretensions to style and their grammatical blunders in Koranic Arabic. He was impressed, however, by French achievements in science and in the administration of justice. Whatever Al-Jabarti may have thought, the British later adapted Napoleon's Egyptian strategic model in their own colonization of Africa, making deft use of anthropologists as instruments of surveillance and subjugation.

If Napoleon's military occupation of Egypt was short-lived, the scientific and scholarly component of his expedition focussed the attention of Europe onto Egypt for the next two centuries. The archeological and scientific data gathered by the scholars of the expedition were compiled into twenty-three massively oversized volumes, called *Descrip-*

tion de l'Égypte. The *Déscription* was published in installments, with the final volume appearing over a decade after
Waterloo. Europe devoured it and the course of European
intellectual history was permanently altered. As Edward
Said has remarked, the *Déscription*, in effect, brought
about, the *invention* of the Orient. More narrowly, the
unearthing of the Rosetta stone during the French occupation made possible the later decipherment of Egyptian
hieroglyphics by Champollion, who had been tutored by
one of the expedition's scholars, Fourier.

Napoleon's conquest of Egypt and his ambitions in the
Middle East and India stirred comparisons with Alexander
the Great and Caesar both in his own mind and in the
European popular mind. It had the effect of transforming
his role from servant of the Directory to its master and
successor on the stage of World History.

One index to that transformation is that from the time
Napoleon returned from Egypt he refused to sit for portraits, though during his rule many paintings of him were
subsequently made. His last portrait sitting, in fact,
occurred on the eve of his departure for Egypt, when he
sat for David for nearly three hours. During the sitting he
challenged David:

What need do you have of a model? Do you believe that the great men of antiquity posed for their portraits? Who troubles to know whether the busts of Alexander resemble him? It is enough that we have an image of him in conformity with his genius. That is how great men must be painted.

Debord, von Clausewitz, and the Game of War

Debord's interest in military history and strategy lead him in 1977 to collaborate with Alice Becker-Ho in creating *The Game of War*. In designing this board game, they intentionally avoided the period reenactments of great battles typical of *Kriegsspiele* in favor of "assembling with the smallest sufficient dimensions of terrain, forces and time, the essentials of the difficulties and the means which may universally be found in the conduct of armies." The rule book for the game, along with a diagrammed account of a match with comments by Debord, was published by Champ Libre in 1987. The basic elements of the game suggest warfare in the Napoleonic era. In the "Preamble" to the rules, Debord explicitly states:

The ensemble of strategic and tactical relationships is summarized in the present Game of War according to the laws set by the theory of Clausewitz, on the basis of the classical warfare of the 18th century, prolonged by the Wars of the Revolution and of the Empire. Thus the nature of the tactical units—on foot or on horseback—, their conventionally fixed offensive and defensive force, the proportion of these various types of units in the army and the support they are capable of bringing, devolve equally from this historical model.

For Debord, the rules of classical warfare—which extend through Napoleon—remain "universal," though "historical," even, as Debord later notes, in light of supervening technological change.

The Game of War functions as a pedagogical synthesis of the military metaphors in Marx and the Situationist practice of the dérive—which expanded Huizinga's notion of the ludic to the experimental defragmentation and reinvention of urban space:

> **dérive:** A mode of experimental behavior linked to the conditions of urban society: a technique of transient passage through varied ambiances. Also used to designate a specific period of continuous dérive.

The importance of play is one of the major currents of Situationist theory and practice. An essay in the first issue of the *Situationist International* journal called "Contribution to a Situationist definition of the game" proposes an outline passing from game as alienated spectacle—spectator sports—to collective participation in a ludic ambiance encompassing all of life lived to the measure of desire: ultimately, the radical overturning of alienated relations of production, the surpassing of the distinction between "work" and "play."

While *The Game of War* is clearly no substitute for that ultimate social transformation, neither is it a commodified "hobby." It is rather a tool for the rehearsal of intelligent large-scale armed insurrection, intended to build strategic habits of mind through practical exercises in military improvisation. Compared to its popular contemporary American formulation of Napoleonic warfare, the game of *Risk*, the Debord and Becker-Ho game is vastly more complex. In *The Game of War*, evaluating lines of communication, geographical position, logistics, and the relative speed and strength of different units all factor into the outcome. In *Risk*, the meaning of geographical position is reduced largely to simple topological adjacency; the concentrated quantities of armies and their offensive or defensive coefficients determine the stochastic representation of their force. Dice are thrown and the final outcome of battle is then determined largely by the law of large numbers. Individual player intervention has fairly minimal effect. *Risk* is, thus, an historical reflection of the global outlook of Cold War technocracy. The statistically-oriented logistical bias of that outlook appears on the horizon of military history as a positivistic misreading of the construct of *Total War*, originally developed by von Clausewitz in theorizing the experience of warfare in his own generation, the age of Napoleon. The contrast between the two games reflects the differences between two opposing readings of von Clausewitz and two opposing designs: *Risk* aims at the formation of detached, interchangeable technocrat-statisticians serving a perdurable National Super State; *The Game of War* aims at the formation of engaged and imaginative individuals capable of strategic planning and practical improvisation in the overturning of existing conditions.

Corpus as corpus delicti

In order to historically position the present edition of Napoleonic maxims, we must consider current English language editions of *The Military Maxims of Napoleon*.

The edition in widest circulation at the present time was produced under the supervision of the prolific British scholar David C. Chandler, head of the Department of War Studies at the Royal Military Academy, Sandhurst. That edition is, in fact, a reprint of the 1901 edition of William E. Cairnes. It contains not only Chandler's introduction and detailed technical tactical commentaries on the maxims, but the entire 1901 edition including the introduction by Cairnes, relating Napoleonic dicta to the recent experience of the Boer War. The translation of the maxims of Napoleon of the Cairnes edition of 1901 is itself a wholesale reprint of the translation of a British colonial army officer, who was a *contemporary* of Napoleon, General Sir George Charles D'Aguilar (1784-1855). The D'Aguilar translation, based on a very incomplete French edition of Napoleonic maxims of 1827, first appeared in *1831*, barely a decade after Napoleon's death.

The only other English language compilation of Napoleonic maxims in current circulation known to me is the one contained in *Roots of Strategy*, (1940) edited by Brg. Gen. T. R. Phillips of the U.S. Army. Though Phillips does not acknowledge this, if we follow the detective work of Cloarec, Phillips seems to have relied exclusively on the edition of Professor L. E. Henry of 1900, which, in turn, derives from the same French edition of 1827—compiled by a General Burnod—that was used by D'Aguilar. The Phillips/Henry version includes the same 78 maxims, though differently translated, as the Chandler/Cairnes edition of the D'Aguilar translation. The Phillips/Henry version, however, is supplemented with 37 additional maxims which comprise a Book Two.

Since the Phillips/Henry edition is the most recent translation, at the very least, nearly a century has passed since the military thought of Napoleon has been retranslated into English. What is more surprising and disturbing is that since *both* the Chandler/Cairnes/D'Aguilar edition *and* the Phillips/Henry edition derive from General Burnod's collection of 1827, no first-hand critical reassessment of Napoleon's thinking on the art of war has been possible for the English-speaking world from 1831 until now.

The net result is that Napoleon's extraordinary reflections on strategy, tactics, the critique of ideology, and the problematic relations of theory and practice have been reduced to a dictionary of received ideas. In the form of presentation and in the ideological ossifications of the commentary attached to them, these insights have been made distant from us as those of the Presocratics, whose fragmentary

magnetism never fails to attract the particles of intellectual detritus necessary to produce a Rorschach blot of an
historical epoch. In assessing our own century, we have
been left up to now, then, with the fuzzy floating illusions
of military-imperial fashion. To cut through that ideological haze, Yann Cloarec, the editor of the current collection
of Napoleon's reflections on the art of war, surveyed the
Napoleonic corpus and strategically reassembled from it
an exquisite and dialectical concentration of forces, to
promote an *active* reading of that missing body of work.

Text: Context

Though he speaks on the subject of warfare with a self-
assurance born of experience and position, Napoleon
never assumes the posture of Philosopher King discours-
ing on glimpses of ideal forms. His gaze is directed
repeatedly and ruthlessly at the world. His sense of contingency, of context, of situation is acute. For him, there
are no eternally fixed rules for the art of war. He repeatedly acknowledges that whatever he may say, there will
always remain something he will be unable to say, not
because the truth is hidden and mystical but because in
war there is no sense in being dead right.

Though he occasionally appeals to the notion of military genius, he makes it clear that "genius" derives from the methodical application of one's "higher lights"; that is, he appeals to Enlightenment intellectual values. "Success in war depends on the prudence, the proper conduct and the experience of the general." "It is a sense of conduct that properly constitutes genius in war." This sense of conduct, however, is learned "neither from books, nor from habit."

For Napoleon, military success on a basic level is more a matter of proportion than of brilliance alone:

> A man of war must have as much character as intelligence; men who have a great deal of intelligence and little character are the least well suited; it is like a ship with masts too far out of proportion with its ballast; it is better to have a great deal of character and little intelligence. Men, who are of but mediocre intelligence and a proportionate character, often succeed in this profession; what is needed is as much base as height. A general who has a great deal of intelligence and character in the same degree—this is Caesar, Hannibal, Prince Eugène, and Frederick.

Great intelligence with little character is the formula for military disaster. The great captains have possessed the unusual combination of breadth of intelligence and breadth of character. While Napoleon is conscious of the rarity of the combination, his analysis consists of the practical application of basic psychology. He insists, however, that

> Generals-in-chief are guided by their own experience or by their genius. Tactics, maneuvers, the science of the engineer and of the artillerist can be learned from treatises more or less like geometry; but knowledge of the higher aspects of war can be acquired only through experience, through the study of the history of wars and of the battles of the great captains. Does one learn by studying grammar how to compose a book of *The Iliad*, a tragedy of Corneille?

Technical training plus experience plus the study of the great captains. A seemingly simple formulation of the relation between theory and practice, yet genius is not identical with experience or learning or a knowledge of historical models alone. His final appeal is to poetry, the terrain of paradox and imagination.

"Nothing can be absolute in war," says Napoleon. In his repeated acknowledgment of contingency, Napoleon is almost alone among those who have commented on the art of war. Vegetius, Machiavelli, even the Maréchal de Saxe and Frederick the Great have been willing to offer fixed prescriptions in their writings for strategy and even for tactics and logistics. Perhaps only Sun Tzu and von Clausewitz are as scrupulous in their attentions to contingency.

Though the fragmentary nature of our encounter with Napoleon's remarks may to some degree enhance this sense of contingency, it is clear that Napoleon was capable of explicitly and consciously contradicting not only received ideas but even his own previous pronouncements in order to convey his meaning at any given moment. His remark that "one fights with cannons as one fights with one's fists" is often quoted even today. Less well known is that Napoleon, aware of the dangers of the blind application of any dictum, also remarked: "Whatever one may say to you, never believe that one fights with cannons as one fights with one's fists. Once firing has commenced, the least shortage of munitions during the action renders useless whatever one had done at the beginning." The application of strong tactics without adequate logistical support is fatal; it is strategy which must provide the insight to balance the two under the constantly changing conditions of battle.

In the second half of this century, a blind faith in technology and mathematical modeling has brought logistics to dominate institutional discourse from business to government to warfare, what Chris Hables Gray describes as "postmodern war." Ironically, at the current time, the most widely read authority on military matters is undoubtedly Sun Tzu, the 5th or 6th century BC strategist and general of the late Classical or early Warring States period in China. Sun Tzu is hardly a believer in conquering by sheer numbers and machines, yet there are some ten widely varying translations of his *Art of War* in print at the moment in English alone. This compares to one or two essentially identical editions of the military maxims of Napoleon, easily the most important military man of the past two centuries in the West. This paradoxical state of affairs is partly due to the inherent interest of Sun Tzu's brilliant observations and partly due to an interest in the successful Asian business strategies allegedly guided by Sun Tzu's strategic wisdom. I would argue that Sun Tzu's acute sense of contingency fills a gap created by the loss of the Napoleonic strategic legacy brought about by its ideological fossilization within western military tradition.

It would seem that 20th century military strategists have either ignored Napoleon or at best relied for their understanding of Napoleonic strategy upon a circuitous and restricted reading of Napoleon's Prussian commentator, von Clausewitz, rather than upon Napoleon himself. To reconstruct this (mis)reading, we might say, that von Clausewitz's emphasis on a systematic approach to his subject is narrowly linked to his theoretical construct of Total War. This forced linkage creates a teleological frame of reference: extreme logistical quantification becomes the methodology for the realization of an *ideology* of Total War. Von Clausewitz's often repeated and widely decontextualized observation that "War is the continuation of Politics by other means" is then taken as a corollary which is understood to mean that military and domestic policy are both best governed by the common denominators of the dictates of accounting. Speer prefigures McNamara. The problem is that this reading minimizes von Clausewitz's account of contingency derived from his own battlefield experience, what he calls *friction*. He admonishes that, "this tremendous friction, which cannot, as in mechanics, be reduced to a few points, is everywhere in contact with chance, and brings about effects that cannot be measured, just because they are largely due to chance." The anecdotal, experiential force of such an observation is invisible to the statistician's mathematical vision of chance as probability.

The ethical limitations of the rule of techno-accountancy in the military show themselves in the moral bankruptcy of the language of "collateral damage" made infamous during the Vietnam War and revived during the Gulf War. The practical limitations of that world view were recently brought to light by an effort undertaken several years ago—at Congressional request and taxpayer expense—by one of the nation's foremost accounting firms to create a model of the Pentagon's accounting system in order to facilitate governmental oversight of military procurement. Within a relatively short time, the firm arrived at the definitive conclusion that the system could not be successfully modeled because it was utterly incoherent. When the balance sheet reaches teratological dimensions, it enters the *Book of Imaginary Beings* housed in the Library of Babel.

In the absence of a more complex and wide-ranging first-hand account of the strategic legacy of Napoleon, what has been preserved has become so encrusted with the detritus of his official interpreters that his profound strategic intelligence has been reduced to a set of obsolete tactical and logistical considerations or to the flatulent after-dinner wisdom which reminds us that "an army travels on its stomach." Napoleonic insights—once restored to their dialectical form—can only help to offset what is so widely perceived as lacking not only in the cadres of commercial and military institutions but in the individuals who would oppose them.

These insights, however, are far from oracular. Napoleon's sense of contingency did not prevent him from viewing the art of war as a highly structured pursuit, resembling higher mathematics or mechanics:

> Every operation should be carried out according to a system, because nothing succeeds by means of chance. In war, nothing is obtained except by calculation; anything which is not deeply thought through in the details never produces any result. In war, simple and precise ideas are needed.

Strategic planning is not only a matter of establishing an optimally linked series of actions on the basis of the best available information, but of taking account of all possible contingencies. As Napoleon himself said, "I shall be accused of temerity, not of slowness, still one must have in one's favor the odds given by calculation." Not even contingency, it seems, is absolute in war.

Watching the detectives

Napoleon informs us that, in order to know when to strike, a commander must keep the battlefield under constant surveillance. He also points to the reciprocal importance of managing how one is perceived by the enemy. That ranges from choices in the physical disposition of troops to hide their numbers, to the control of information in the press, to the use of spies, the interrogation of prisoners, the intercepting of mail, and finally to the strategic advantages conferred by promoting and maintaining a strong reputation in arms.

In order to know when to strike in the domestic sphere, Napoleon approved the recruitment of the master criminal Vidocq—on Vidocq's own initiative—as the head of a special unit within the national police, the Brigade de Sûreté. Vidocq, who was actually in jail at time of his appointment, in turn, employed only ex-criminals in his élite corps of criminal investigators. In the course of his service to the State, Vidocq revolutionized police work. He concentrated an extraordinary attention to detail on the investigation of crime scenes. He invented the police line up and the practice of keeping permanent records on felons. Bertillon, who introduced the system of physical classification of criminals in police work, which ultimately led to the introduction of fingerprinting, named Vidocq as his inspiration.

After an illustrious and sensational public career, Vidocq left government service under a cloud of suspicion. By that point, however, he had managed to extend his career not only beyond Napoleon's Empire, but some 10 years beyond the end of Napoleon's life. Immediately upon his return to private life, he established the first private detective agency. Unlike Sam Spade, his principal occupation was to offer protective services and security advice to businesses. He quickly found himself in conflict with the State by offering a challenge to its well-known and jealously guarded monopoly over the "protection" of its citizens.

Vidocq's legacy, however, extends well beyond the purely professional. Balzac modeled Vautrin of the *Comédie Humaine* upon him. Poe evokes his name and reputation in the unraveling of the bizarre enigma of the "Murders of the Rue Morgue," one of the earliest detective stories. An autobiography of Vidocq—now thought to be a fake—has been a perennial favorite in France. In the past few years, his notorious life provided the basis for a popular television series and a best-selling novel in France.

The story of Vidocq is bound up inextricably with Napoleon's complex understanding of the strategic value of surveillance. The application of the paradoxical strategy of repressing criminality, through the employment of the most expert of criminal minds, constituted the foundation of the police apparatus of the modern State and the detective genre which sings its arms and its men.

Strategy and tactics

Some military usage refers to campaign plans and battle plans; Napoleon refers as well to the *system* for a campaign and for a battle. The distinction separating plan from system seems to parallel the one separating tactics from strategy. If tactics or plans may be thought of as sets of procedures to be carried out, then strategy or system comprises the rules which govern the applications of those procedures according to the variations of conditions. But since tactics develop and evolve from battlefield experience, they must ultimately inform strategy—if it is to be successful long-term—in a dynamic, dialectical relationship rather than a purely static hierarchical one. Though some have qualified him as being more gifted as a strategist than a tactician, Napoleon's grasp of the complex interactions of strategy and tactics may be the source of what is often referred to as the emperor's superb sense of timing. "One must be slow in deliberations and quick in execution" he admonishes.

Napoleon's commentaries on the chain of command reflect parallel insights and difficulties. Orders are never to be blindly followed, he tells us. The commander in the field must never carry out an order from headquarters that he believes will have disastrous consequences. He is *obliged* to use his own judgment, to ask for explanations, and to resign rather than to obey any order he knows will bring the ruin of his men. Nor is the commander-in-chief required to obey the orders of a minister or prince distant from the scene of battle, when those orders contradict his own better judgment. Individual responsibility and judgment close the critical feedback loop of theory and practice, strategy and tactics. And of course, Napoleon contradicts himself: "An order must always be executed. When it is not, a crime takes place, and the guilty must be punished." And he carefully—if awkwardly—resolves the matter by contradicting this apparent contradiction: "A military order itself does not require a passive obedience except when it is given by a superior, who, being present at the moment he gives it, has a knowledge of the state of things, can listen to the objections and give explanations to the one who should execute the order." For Napoleon, it is ultimately the general-in-chief who must resolve all such contradictions on the basis of his superior, global viewpoint and give orders. "There is no need to say what one has the intention of doing at the same moment that one does it."

The importance of understanding the complex nature of the relationship between strategy and tactics may be appreciated by again considering the consequences of the translation of military metaphors into the social, economic and political spheres. Napoleon sustained his years of power, not only by understanding the relationship of tactics and strategy, but by systematically organizing European politics according to the values he had learned in the military sphere of thorough and dispassionate planning:

> The character of our nation is to be far too lively in prosperity. If we take as a basis of all operations true politics, which is nothing but the calculation of combinations and of odds, we will be for a long time the great nation and the arbiter of Europe. I say further: we hold the balance of Europe; we shall make it incline as we wish and, if such be the order of destiny, I see no impossibility in our achieving with-

> in a few years even those great results that the heated and enthusiastic imagination half-glimpses, and that the man who is extremely cold, constant and rational, will alone attain.

Applying the same dispassionate standards to Napoleon himself, his downfall might be attributed to that same heated and enthusiastic imagination. More mundane critics—pointing to the disasters of the Russian Campaign and minimizing the unorthodox successes of the Italian Campaign—have attributed that downfall to inadequate attention to the domain of logistics, the branch of military science concerned with procurement, supply and maintenance of equipment, the movement of personnel, and the provisioning of facilities and related matters.

Our own century, as Manfredo Tafuri has pointed out, has been dominated by the plan. The inflexible and militant scientism of the "Soviet" bureaucrats and their procrustean 5-year plans created murderous wastes of scarce human and material resources. While observing that inflexible State planning may have ultimately contributed to the collapse of the "evil empire," we must also remember our own incoherent Pentagon accounting system. And we must reflect even more carefully on the smiley-faced scenarios of the Reagan/Bush/Clinton End of History. A glimpse in that privatized funhouse mirror, reveals the ideological domination of multi-national capitalism and the nomadic MBA's and political subalterns who service it by the quarterly business plan. Having largely abandoned long-term strategic planning, management has retreated to shorter and shorter functional units, more amenable to purely tactical, numerically manageable interventions. This form of Economics prides itself on having severed its connection with the larger dimensions of History, to exist almost purely in the present. But the abandonment of long term strategic values means the abandonment of shared cultural values. This is the cost of a belief in the End of History: a hierarchical domination of tactics by logistics has largely displaced the complex interactions of logistics and tactics mediated by strategy. While this pseudo-seasonal variability has proved adaptable if not infallible on fiscal terrain, it threatens long-term growth by jeopardizing basic research, for basic research cannot be directly tied to quarterly profits, domestic or military. On the level of sociology, it destroys institutional loyalty by eliminating job security. In the wake of this trend to privilege short term logistical considerations over long term development strategy, we are witnessing a pyrrhic implosion of social subjects. Anyone who doubts the depth of the impact has only to remember that in the United States at least even junior high school students are now going postal. Piratical upward shifts of wealth crown its short-term "victories" at the expense of the vanishing "public sector." Even in the newly former "Soviet" Union, many express a nostalgia for the social coherence of the days of Stalin—as their forebears had earlier expressed a nostalgia for the days of the tsar. Russian government officials at the highest level publicly acknowledge the loss of shared goals, ikons and values, finding themselves incapable of proposing adequate official substitutes as the state monopoly over the protection racket is privatized.

In the U.S., as short term cost-benefit analysis replaces social ethics, we are witnessing the destruction not only of the social service institutions of the "welfare state" but also the educational, cultural and research institutions that shape shared values, drive the high technology at the base of current relations of production and train technical cadres, the need for which has become so great they must currently be imported. Not only is the public educational system under attack by various competing ideologies, but the lordlings of Silicon Valley are notoriously ungenerous—compared not only to pragmatic Rockefeller Republicans but to the robber barons of the industrial revolution—in their paltry contributions to public and private "charity." Even the symbolic prestige derived from the public destruction of wealth—the *potlatch* principle exemplified by the Getty Museum—is lost on these technologues.

As Science becomes increasingly privatized and militarized, it is reduced to the technical means of extracting profits for dealing death. Leaving aside purely ethical considerations, this designation of Science as the direct servant of the military industrial complex is of questionable historical wisdom, for it was the relatively unrestricted research efforts of NASA that supplied the critical catalysts for current developments in information technology from the personal computer to virtual reality. One can only wonder at the great results the heated and enthusiastic imagination of a Bill Gates—the self-declared salesman of obsolescence—half glimpses, when we have seen the kitsch post-historical social vision of a Newt Gingrich.

Within the corporate welfare state, the military has become the remaining though unacknowledged and self-perpetuating "public sector." Spectacular evidence of this institutional momentum may be seen in the technophiliac propaganda of the Gulf War. Sophisticated, expert-directed campaigns not only substituted aestheticized remote-controlled explosions for ethical judgments, but grossly exaggerated the technological efficacy of the weapons systems involved. Iraqi civilian casualties were rendered invisible by effective monopolization of broadcast bandwidth. Record ratings were the ironic, tautological proof of the existence of a closed system conducting a saturation bombing of domestic consciousness simultaneously with the strategic "real world" destruction of exotic locales.

"Be all that you can be!" echoes bitterly as the drastic cutbacks in the scope of educational and job-training programs and unemployment benefits have reduced the universe of possibilities for many to MacDonald's, workfare, or the Army. The rise of the corporate welfare state and the social stratification it entails has directly fueled the desperate flight of individuals as well as state and local governments towards lotteries and casino gambling. Pseudo-symbolic economic exchange has replaced policies based on rational attempts to ensure general economic well-being through limited redistribution of wealth. The fantasy of social agency and economic mobility has been transformed to the intervention of the unseen hand of a rigorously stochastic market, with the state taking a cut behind the scenes. In a striking return of the politically repressed, the sovereignty of Native Americans has found its first major economic engine—since the rise of the exploitation of mineral resources—in reservation gambling. The occupation of a critical marginality as a sovereign state within the larger prison of the state has produced a golden opportunity or golden welfare for a limited number of the descendants of the survivors of the genocide which cleared the way for the paradigmatic and oxymoronic Universal Nation State.

Translation and betrayal

Because Napoleon's impact on the textuality of history is so vast, the strategies of this translation have been devised to shape that historicity in several ways. The guiding principle for this translation has been to stay as close to both the syntax and the vocabulary of the original text as possible without destroying its meaning. I have attempted, somewhat polemically, to follow the indications of Walter Benjamin in his essay on the task of the translator, to allow the original text to shine through. I have tried to be consistent as possible in translating terms used repeatedly in the text. This effort has produced somewhat paradoxical results in the case of two particular terms: "politique" and "avant-garde."

"La politique" in French governs a range of meanings

which joins two terms usually seen as distinct in contemporary American usage: "politics" and "policy." "Policy" reflects the perspective of the party in power, as in "foreign policy." "Politics" reflects a larger perspective, including not only that of the opposition party in so-called representative democracy, but one that extends beyond the End of History repeatedly proclaimed by the revolutions of the last 200 years. Politics, we might say, is the continuation of war by other means. In order to preserve the anti-ideological character of Napoleon's thought in the form of its original statement, I have chosen to translate "politique" more often by "politics" or "a politics," less often by "policy."

In contemporary American English, the term "avant-garde" suggests a cultural frame of reference. In French, "avant-garde" retains both military and cultural connotations. It is often rendered in English by "advance guard" or "vanguard." Though "vanguard" might effect a more transparent compromise, I have chosen the term "avant-garde" even in a military context—as did Coleridge, Napoleon's contemporary—in order to bring forth an active, critical and historical reading of the text.

While Napoleon speaks from the perspective of one who

rules, his perspective extends beyond the boundaries of bourgeois ideology—though in which historical direction one may indeed question. I would like to suggest a reading of Napoleon that recalls the practice of Soviet intellectuals of the 1920's in reading D. W. Griffith. They absorbed both his formal innovations and his anti-capitalist perspective, though the latter derived as much from Griffith's nostalgia for his aristocratic Southern upbringing as from any higher sense of social justice. We must weigh in the same balance *A Corner in Wheat* and *Birth of a Nation*. We must consider that Napoleon was capable of flouting the Vatican, despising the bourgeoisie and bringing reforms in the feudal relations of master and serf as he was of restoring religion as a mechanism of social control, ennobling the bourgeoisie as subalterns to his imperial dynasty, and abolishing the Revolution's guarantees against slavery to promote French colonialism.

One final term deserves mention: "coup d'oeil." It appears only in section III, maxim 63. I have rendered it as "sweep of vision." The French suggests, first, a physical "sweep of the eye, " a scanning, a glance. More importantly, at stake is the ability of a commander to take in an entire scene, to understand the *significance* of the physical dispositions and movements of troops "at a glance," a higher cognitive rather than a purely retinal function. It carries this intellectual significance in French beyond a strictly military context.

I mention this term because I believe it is important *not* to fall into the technological determinism of Paul Virilio in his analysis of Griffith and Napoleon in *Cinema and War*. For, if Napoleon and D. W. Griffith hold in common a certain understanding of the *techné* of vision, which depends upon the single vanishing point perspective of an early 19th century artilleryman's geometry, they both also understood that history is a matter of contingency. It requires—for both its production and reproduction on a mass-scale—complex, advance planning as well as constant improvisation. Though Griffith's optical and geometrical understandings of the battlefield were circumscribed by the rules of linear perspective, he knew that the frame alone does not make the shot, nor the sequence, nor the film. Griffith was one of the most radical innovators in the narrative tradition in his use of the cross-cutting of parallel action; his sweep of vision made possible a greater understanding of the construction of history and story. He was the author not only of *Birth of a Nation*, but of *Intolerance*. Napoleon, we might say, also scripted things tightly, but because shooting out of sequence, retakes and post-production are impossible on the battlefield—just to torture the analogy to death—he was forced to master in-camera editing and this requires as much planning as improvisation.

I am no longer Virilio

Virilio and some of his less imaginative admirers have recently assumed post-historical postures of positively Hegelian ambition. For them, military technology determines History, and as we approach war at the speed of light—pure war—we effectively reach the End of History. What underlies this project, however, is the simple desire to become reconciled with these dazzling shifts in technology. To paraphrase Debord, *the paradox which consists in suspending the meaning of all history in favor of its technological accomplishment, and in revealing this meaning at the same time by constituting itself as the accomplishment of technology, devolves from the simple fact that the thinker of the technological revolutions of the 20th century has sought in his philosophy only reconciliation with their result.* As a side-effect, history itself is reconceived as a form of technology, an intellectual technology of time, privileging the synchronic over the diachronic. In linguistic terms, this loss of narrative in favor of the luminous fragment might be compared to the pathological condition of contiguity disorder where the sentence becomes reduced to a sparkling word heap.

The alternative is not to ignore technology in theorizing history, but to understand the relationship between observation and participation. Aphasia, metaphor and dialectics exist along a continuum. In terms of cyber discourse, we might say that while the special effects of inter-passivity should not be underestimated, Virilio's techno-determinism amounts to the abandonment of a theory based on social practice, in favor of a death obsessed variant of the feel-ecstatic passivity of the utopian post-historicism known as the "Californian ideology." Virilio's apocalyptic vision reconciles his own Christian millennialism and oedipal anti-communism in a technologically induced ecstasy of speed.

It is significant that Virilio evokes the paradigm of Napoleonic insanity to describe what he calls the de-realization caused by virtual reality:

> Imagine that all of a sudden I am convinced that I am Napoleon: I am no longer Virilio, but Napoleon. My reality is wounded. Virtual reality leads to a similar de-realization. However, it no longer works

only at the scale of individuals, as in madness, but
at the scale of the world.

Napoleon's world historical ambitions and achievements
are here a negative stereotype of political agency—radical
subjectivity—the ironic exception which proves the rule
of individual political impotence. Virilio offers a fable of
failed omniscience and omnipotence, that sees the ambition of becoming a world historical subject as a descent
into madness. He then tells us that virtual reality univer-
salizes a failed and illusory subjecthood as if that settled
the matter. The choice is rather whether to accept the
socialization of that pseudo-agency or to understand that
virtual reality—as he broadly defines it—is but another
aspect of the integrated spectacle and to resist it. "Tactical
media" has been one effort in this direction. It remains to
be seen whether in practice tactical media will bring forth
any social configuration of the importance of the soviet—
or even the dérive—as a laboratory of political agency.
The coordinated, yet decentralized Zapatista browser
attacks show a promising direction in the continuation of
politics by other means.

In fairness, Virilio is aware of the difficulties of his positions for activities of resistance. He has acknowledged an

involuntary identification on his part with the military institutions whose power he describes and avers to detest. He has even expressed admiration for local efforts of popular defense against the expanding machinery of pure war. He remains oddly perplexed, however, that such popular struggles can coexist with—let alone flourish against—the juggernaut of superior military technology and has actively dissociated himself from the autonomist practice inspired by an anti-authoritarian reading of his work.

Theory: Practice

Napoleon observes that, "The theory is not the practice of war" and Debord that "The soviet was not a discovery of theory." Theorist Frederic Jameson, the critic of various totalizing "master narratives" including, it would seem, the narrative of History itself, once flatly pronounced the Situationist International "a failure." Although Jameson did not elaborate on the basis for this master theoretical pronouncement, giving him the wide theoretical berth he would claim, it seems fair to say that Jameson was unaware that Debord had already formulated an active and historical response to the question of evaluating the role of the Situationist International in the historical movement which culminated in the May '68 uprising. In the final minutes of his film, *Society of the Spectacle*, Debord observes in a title card:

> "It would obviously be very convenient to make history if one had only to engage in struggle under unerringly favorable circumstances." To completely destroy this society, it is clearly necessary to be ready to launch against it, ten times in succession or more, assaults of an importance comparable to that of May 1968; and to hold as inevitable inconveniences a certain number of defeats and civil wars. The goals which count in universal history must be affirmed with energy and will.

If there is little to expect even in theory from those whose horizons are bounded by theory alone, there are other difficulties in adapting the observations of Napoleon or the Situationists to the current arena of social struggle. Napoleon complained about the lack of useful historical accounts of the Wars of the Revolution; the same complaint could be made concerning the lack of useful historical accounts of the social warfare of 1968, either in France or elsewhere. Though excellent in other ways, both Viénet's and Dumontier's accounts of May '68, for example, assume, and therefore leave unrecounted, accessible basic narratives of the events, of the dispositions and movements of the forces in the streets.

To find our bearings in the labyrinths of this century, we might do well to reexamine not only the psychogeographical maps left by Debord and the Situationists, but also what remains of the efforts of August von Cieszkowski and the Young Hegelians. Von Cieszkowski's *Prolegomena to Historiosophy*, originally published in 1838, seems to have had a decisive influence on Debord's account of the role of the Situationist International in May of '68. A French translation of the *Prolegomena* was published in April 1973 by Champ Libre, only months before Debord began work on his film version of *Society of the Spectacle*. Debord quotes a rather difficult passage from it in a title card early in the film:

> Thus, after the immediate practice of art has ceased to be what is most eminent and this predicate has devolved to theory as such, it separates itself for the present from this latter, to the degree that synthetic post-theoretical praxis is constituted, which has first as its mission to be the foundation and truth of art as of philosophy.

Debord's act of citation serves to historically position his own work: his film is not an intellectual project in the service of revolution, rather it constitutes an exemplary form of post-theoretical synthetic praxis. There is an instructive parallel in the ambitions of the Anglo-American Conceptual Art movement to produce—in the phrase of Joseph Kosuth—Art after [the demise in the 20th century of] Philosophy. But the difference is even more instructive. While the Situationists sought a synthesis of Art, Philosophy, and Politics, aimed at the overturning of existing society and all its categories, Conceptual Artists remained content to explode the received categories of "objecthood" of the domain of high art, while remaining firmly within it. In their assault on the institutional fortresses of the gallery-magazine-museum system, they deployed an aggressive scientistic philosophical discourse based on the positivistic methodology of American social science and on the mandarin terminological proliferations of the Philosophy of Language known as Logical Positivism. By effectively producing a hybrid form of art criticism as art, they gained access to the heart of the citadel in order to occupy it themselves, not to destroy it. While attempts to market their documentation within the gallery system as rare manuscripts met with some limited success, their contributions ultimately became a sub-genre of art historical literature. Since the gallery system survives on marketing luxury commodities, as the market lost interest, almost all Conceptual Artists were dropped from the system. In order to continue their efforts, some retreated into painting and sculpture—the forbidden domain of objecthood—occasionally producing written statements; some moved exclusively into literature; some moved into film and video; some ceased art making altogether. While there are myriad contradictions on both sides, comparing the Situationists with Conceptual Artists, we are confronted with two decidedly different understandings of the phrase "occupations movement." Only Henry Flynt—the originator of the term Concept Art—and his associates Tony Conrad and Jack Smith maintained extended offensives against "serious culture." While their their deadpan street protests managed to infect the complacent air around cultural institutions, they never coalesced—and the question is open whether they were ever meant to— with popular uprisings.

For the professional intellectual of the present, the Barthesian assurance that in offering cultural criticism, one wears the hat of both artist and critic, currently serves only to maintain a dandified complacency. The social effect—or the lack of it—of intellectual work remains effectively outside of consideration, because it remains within its own self-imposed ghetto. The author defines himself or herself as a "producer" only while remaining securely within quotation marks.

Postface in the guise of an obsessively repeated personal anecdote

When I was in the fourth grade, I wrote my only short story. The story was written with a ball-point pen in blue ink on both sides of a single sheet of Nifty™ notebook paper. A drawing at the bottom of the back of the sheet illustrated its apocalyptic conclusion.

The story began: "I am Anon von Giets, Scientist." That name (pronounced "ah-non von jeets") was a complex anagram of my own name, "anonymous," "Werner von Braun," and the name of the most popular kid in my class. With a Hollywood German accent, this voice recounted a scenario in which every scrap of information I had ever encountered on War was treated as a variable to be incorporated in the solution of a monstrous simultaneous equation derived by the inexorable psychic apparatus of my Catholic upbringing.

First, I invented a huge computer with the capacity to produce robots. I commanded it to build an army of robots, each with the capacity to build other robots. My legions multiplied exponentially and I easily took over the world. Next, I commanded my robots to build space-ships and sent them to take over the Universe. Finally—realizing that the common error of Hitler, Napoleon, and Julius Caesar was not strategic geographic overextension (as everyone else seemed to think) but rather the failure to consider to the fullest the dimension of Time, that is to say, History—I commanded my robots to build a time machine and sent endless legions into both the entire past and the entire future. The last line of the story reads: "Now, I am Master of the Universe! Past, Present, and to Come!"

* * *

I would like to thank all those who contributed to this translation and essay. First, Pascale-Anne Brault, whose meticulous reading of one of my early "final" drafts, improved both the accuracy of the translation and the quality of the English. Jon Burris, Vincent Grenier, Geneviève Hayes, Catherine Ruello, and John Reese Thomas provided additional suggestions for the translation. Robert Cowley kindly provided me with information concerning the history of military technology and terminology. Craig Baldwin, Tom Damrauer, John Dougan, Wendy Dougan, Barbara Lattanzi, Laura Lindgren, Chuck Mee, Julie Murray, Ken Swezey and my father provided information, advice and encouragement at various stages of the process. Diane Bertolo made numerous important contributions to the final shape of the book. And finally, to Peggy Ahwesh I owe a debt I find impossible to justly express. None of these individuals should, of course, be held accountable for my interpretations of their suggestions.

New York, 1998

A supplemental account of Napoleon I,
Emperor of the French,
in the form of
an historical and comparative
compilation of citations
accompanied by related illustrations
inspired by the life and work of
Walter Benjamin and
Bouvard and Pécuchet.

I saw the Emperor—that Worldsoul—riding out to reconnoiter the city; it is truly a wonderful sensation to see such an individual, concentrated here on a single point, astride a single horse, yet reaching across the world and ruling it . . . To make such progress from Thursday to Monday is possible only for this extraordinary man, whom it is impossible not to admire.

Georg Wilhelm Friedrich Hegel
Letter to Niethammer, October 13, 1806
translated by Joachim Neugroschel

It is clear, consequently, that war is not a mere act of policy but a true political instrument, a continuation of political activity by other means. What remains peculiar to war is simply the peculiar nature of its means. War in general, and the commander in any specific instance, is entitled to require that the trend and designs of policy shall not be inconsistent with these means. That, of course, is no small demand; but however much it may affect political aims in a given case, it will never do more than modify them. The political object is the goal, war is the means of reaching it, and means can never be considered in isolation from their purpose.

Carl von Clausewitz
***On War*, 1830**
translated by Michael Howard and Peter Paret

We—the artists—will be your avant-garde. The power of the arts is in effect the most immediate and most rapid of all powers. We have all kinds of weapons. When we wish to spread new ideas among men, we inscribe them on marble or canvas; we popularize them in poetry and song; we use, in turn, the lyre or the tabor, the ode or the ballad, the story or the novel; the drama is open to us, and through it, above all, we are able to exercise an electric and victorious influence. We address ourselves to man's imagination and sentiments; consequently we are always bound to have the sharpest and most decisive effect.

Henri Saint-Simon and Léon Halévy
The Artist, the Scientist and the Industrial:
***dialogue*, 1825**
translated by Keith Taylor, slightly altered.

It has, then, been proved that the supposed hero of our century is nothing more than an allegorical personage, deriving his attributes from the sun. It follows that Napoleon Bonaparte, of whom so much has been said and written, never even existed; and this fallacy, into which so many people have fallen headlong, arises from the amusing blunder of mistaking the mythology of the nineteenth century for history.

Jean-Baptiste Pérès
"The Grand Erratum. The Non-existence of Napoleon proved," 1827 in *The Napoleon Myth*, edited by Henry Ridgely Evans, 1904.
translated by 'Lily'

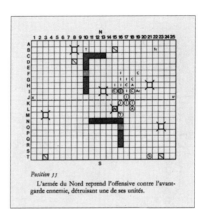

Position 55

L'armée du Nord reprend l'offensive contre l'avant-
garde ennemie, détruisant une de ses unités.

The same spirit of analytical investigation which creates a theory should also guide the work of the critic who both may and should often cross into the realm of theory in order to elucidate any points of special importance. The function of criticism would be missed entirely if criticism were to degenerate into a mechanical application of theory. All the positive results of theoretical investigation—all the principles, rules, and methods—will increasingly lack universality and absolute truth the closer they come to being positive doctrine. They are there to be used when needed, and their suitability in any given case must always be a matter of judgment. A critic should never use the results of theory as laws and standards, but only—as the soldier does—*as aids to judgment.*

Carl von Clausewitz
***On War,* 1830**
translated by Michael Howard and Peter Paret

The Whole revolutionary work of modern times was symboli-
cally summed up by the Napoleonic substitution of the *Star
of Honor* for the Cross of St. Louis. It was the Pentagram substituted for the Labarum, the reinstatement of the symbol of
light, the Masonic resurrection of Adon-hiram. It is said that
Napoleon believed in his *star*; and therefore he was in the
right to adopt for his sign the Pentagram, that symbol of
human sovereignty by the intelligent initiative.

Eliphas Lévi
***Dogme et rituel de la haute magie*, 1861 quoted by
Henry Ridgely Evans in "The Mythical Napoleon.
An Occult Study" in *The Napoleon Myth*, edited by
Evans, 1904**

...Those who believe in the reincarnations of the soul upon the earth, like the Theosophists, will perhaps endeavor to show that Napoleon was identical with Ramses II. (the Sesotris of the Greeks), with Alexander the Great, and also with Charlemagne. Let us see where this bizarre fancy may lead us.

Henry Ridgely Evans
"The Mythical Napoleon. An Occult Study."
in *The Napoleon Myth*, edited by Evans, 1904

Action in war is like movement in a resistant element. Just as the simplest and most natural of movements, walking, cannot easily be performed in water, so in war it is difficult for normal efforts to achieve even moderate results. A genuine theorist is like a swimming teacher, who makes his pupils practice motions on land that are meant to be performed in water. To those who are not thinking of swimming the motions will appear grotesque and exaggerated. By the same token, theorists who have never swum, or who have not learned to generalize from experience, are impractical and even ridiculous: they teach only what is already common knowledge: how to walk.

Carl von Clausewitz
On War, **1830**
translated by Michael Howard and Peter Paret

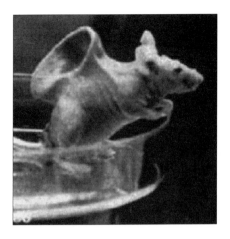

In a famous letter...Hegel says that having finished the *Phenomenology*, he saw at dawn "the soul of the world" ride on horseback under his window. This text is revealing. The victor of Jena is called in it "the soul of the world": he is *Welt*-seele, and not *Volks*-seele; he incorporates not the history of the French people, but that of the whole of humanity. But he is Welt-*seele* and not Welt-*geist*. He is not Spirit, because he is not fully self-conscious; through his actions he in fact completes history, but he does not know that he is doing this and that he realizes absolute Spirit by doing it. It is Hegel who knows this and who says it in the *Phenomenology*. Absolute Spirit or "God" is therefore neither Napoleon nor Hegel, but Napoleon-understood-by-Hegel or Hegel-understanding-Napoleon.

Alexandre Kojève
"Hegel, Marx and Christianity," August/September 1946
translated by Hilail Gildin

I, Bonaparte, am not alone! I had been assisted at that time by those forces with whom I had aligned myself, and who were passengers on this great ship of life, themselves taking commanding roles as members of this party. The ship of state is the very ship that has contained upon it the very same individuals, although the ship may have changed from one life to the next. We will see this in the sailing ship, the ships of the Vikings, the galleys of the English, the French steamships, atomic-powered ships, and indeed spaceships that plied the great open seas between planets! These were the ships that were captained by Bonaparte in previous lives, assisted by many who were those individuals who formed the basis of the French Empire, a republic supposedly to free man from the odorous weight of high taxes, uncivilized order between the many elements of the populations, the imbalances of justice, the complete and total lack of consideration to the individual as a particle of the infinite substance.

The very act of placing the crown on the head of Bonaparte was, in every respect, an immediate attunement to that time when Bonaparte was crowned the Emperor Tyrantus in the far-away planet similar in all respects to the Earth, but dissimilar in respect to its technological development...

This act of Napoleon carried within him a fire which, previous to this time, was tempered to some degree by his concern for and desire to compensate for, and rectify the imbalance of previous acts which had been carried out by him in previous lives in which he had lived as a general of the army and an administrator of his country.

Louis Spiegel (Antares)
I, Bonaparte An Autobiography, **1985**

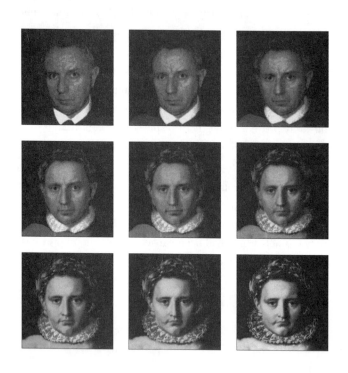

Imagine that all of a sudden I am convinced that I am Napoleon: I am no longer Virilio, but Napoleon. My reality is wounded. Virtual reality leads to a similar de-realization. However, it no longer works only at the scale of individuals, as in madness, but at the scale of the world.

Paul Virilio
"Cyberwar, God and Television: an interview
with Louise Wilson" *CTheory*, **1996**
translated by Gildas Illien